CANDLELIGHT ROMANCE

CANDLELIGHT ROMANCES

LOVE ISLAND

Barbara Max

A CANDLELIGHT ROMANCE

Published by
Dell Publishing Co., Inc.
1 Dag Hammarskjold Plaza
New York, New York 10017

Dell ® TM 681510, Dell Publishing Co., Inc.

ISBN: 0-440-14709-3

Printed in the United States of America

First printing—March 1981

Chapter One

Angela sat on the front porch, tensely waiting for Rory to pick her up and to take her bowling. Her thoughts were racing furiously on this warm June evening, and she watched the fireflies flickering like brief, tantalizing flames without really seeing them.

Today she had received a letter from her best friend, Stephanie Pallas. Angela had not seen her former Greek roommate since their graduation from college two years before, and now Stephanie had invited her to spend the summer in Greece.

Angela's first impulse was to accept immediately, for the prospect greatly excited her. Her life was progressing smoothly but predictably. Angela enjoyed her new independence resulting from her teaching job at the local school. Although she still mourned her dear aunt, who had raised her, Angela and her younger sister, Nancy, lived companionably in the white frame house left to them by their parents in Springport, Massachusetts.

Not only was Angela popular with her friends but she had been engaged for the past eight months to the most eligible young man in town. Rory Martin was rapidly becoming a successful lawyer, and Angela was grateful that his well-to-do family had not offered the slightest objection to his engagement to an orphan who was virtually penniless.

Angela sighed deeply as she thought of her impending marriage. She couldn't actually say why she was so uneasy. She had known Rory from childhood and had always supposed herself in love with him. Everybody in town thought that Angela Blair and Rory Martin were made for each other. They even looked alike, people always remarked, with their corn-colored silky hair and blue eyes.

"Angie? You seem a million miles away," said Rory.

Angela started, suddenly noticing Rory silhouetted against the evening sky. Jumping up, she kissed him, feeling guilty for her disloyal thoughts. If she went to Greece for the summer, she would be parted from Rory, and she surely didn't want that, did she?

Angela remained preoccupied all evening, mechanically going through the motions of bowling, and barely noticing that she had scored strike after strike. Naturally graceful and skilled at sports, Angela had always performed effortlessly and well. Tonight, however, instead of seeing the bowling pins and the alley, she was visualizing ancient marble monuments illuminated by moonlight, and olive trees swaying in the wind. Angela simply couldn't turn off her imagination.

Increasingly of late she had been feeling almost like a bystander in her own life, looking at it from afar as a stranger might see it.

Angela attempted to assess her fiancé objectively. Tall and slim, he was considered quite handsome, although in truth Angela would have said that he had a pleasant, clean-cut face, with regular features. Secretly it upset her to think that others considered her to be almost his mirror image. Surely her face had more—character. When she looked at herself in the mirror, she couldn't see any but the most superficial resemblance of coloring. Her large, slightly oblique

6

eyes were violet-blue and framed by thick golden lashes that looked too abundant to be real. Her nose was fine-boned and her full lips beautifully shaped. Conventional prettiness? But wasn't there an inkling of her vivid imagination, of her curiosity and restlessness beneath the shyness?

Angela's female drama teacher at college had observed that she exuded an intriguing air of mystery, making people wish to fathom her secret warmth and glowing poise. Trying to convince Angela to study drama seriously, her teacher had assured her that when she smiled her face was suffused with a brilliance that dazzled. Angela had grown embarrassed at such praise, and in any case, had not wished to become an actress.

The trouble with Angela at this point was that she wasn't sure what she wanted. Hadn't she always expected to marry Rory and settle down in the nice house his parents would buy for them, have a couple of children, and live happily ever after? Most of Angela's college classmates had already married. Then why not she? Rory was kind, thoughtful, unaffected, and serious. Angela certainly felt comfortable with him, and he was as familiar and cozy as her old cardigan.

Dreamy and restless, Angela's mind kept wandering, and she hardly heard any of the conversation going on around her.

Although Angela had the entire summer off, Rory allowed himself only two weeks each August. For the past two summers, she had been trying to get him to agree to a trip to Europe, but Rory had always balked, "We can't. I can't jeopardize several important cases I have coming up. There will be lots of time later for us to travel and see the world." She had had to conceal her disappointment and pretend great enthusiasm for the camping trips they took instead.

When Rory brought her home that night, she was

still in conflict over the letter from Stephanie. Her friend wrote the way she spoke, with a great rush of enthusiasm.

You must come, Angela, I won't take no for an answer. I enjoyed your hospitality at all the holidays and now it is time for you to enjoy mine. Not to let a Greek reciprocate when we invented the idea in the first place, why that's a crime! I will show you all Athens, and we will cruise the Aegean in our yacht, winding up on our private island.

How Angela's imagination was struck by the picture Stephanie painted! She had read widely about Greece, finding her lively friend's passion for the place contagious. When Angela thought of the Pallas's private island, she grew almost sick with longing. They were a very rich family, Angela knew, prominent in publishing. She was sure the island was gorgeous. Stephanie, whose exuberance sometimes hid a surprising sensitivity, had found a further means of inducing Angela to come to Greece. Knowing that her friend had little money, Stephanie had suggested that Angela teach her small niece and nephew English for a very generous salary.

"Angie, for pete's sake, tell me what is preoccupying you," Rory now requested, gazing at her with his frank blue eyes.

Angela flushed slightly. "I'm sorry, Rory. You're right. I—I have been far away." She told him about Stephanie's letter. Although trying to keep her tone neutral, she couldn't hide the excitement in her voice.

Rory heard it at once. "You want to go, Angie, don't you?" he asked evenly.

She hesitated. "Well, I have missed Stephanie terribly these past two years. And—and if I could actually earn some money—Oh, Rory, couldn't you possibly close the office and come with me?"

"No, I'm afraid that's out of the question. Actually, I sort of thought we might be getting married this summer, and go away for our honeymoon—though not to Europe." Rory looked at Angela reproachfully, and she felt her heart lurch guiltily.

"I—you've been very patient, and I don't blame you for—for wanting to make plans—" Angela trailed off. Could she honestly agree to marry this very summer? It was so soon . . . so final.

Rory continued to gaze at her steadily. "I'm not trying to push you, honey, but if we're going to get married, I think we should set a date."

"But—but Nancy is still so young to be left on her own—"

"Of course she is, but she would live with us, Angie. You know how much I like Nancy."

It was true. Rory had always been wonderful to her sister, and Angela knew she was only stalling. The realization made her feel panicky.

Rory took her hands in his own. "If you really want to visit Stephanie, tell me truthfully."

Angela forced herself to meet Rory's probing eyes. "Yes," she blurted out. "Yes, I do, but—" She stopped then. Were there really any buts?

"I'll tell you what," said Rory, adopting his lawyer's stance. "Why don't you go to Greece for a month? That should satisfy your wanderlust. Then, when you come back at the beginning of August, we can be married and go on our honeymoon. I've got my eye on a secluded cottage on the Cape . . ."

While he spoke, Angela's heart began to do flips. Oh, how she wanted to go to Greece!! Even a month would be heavenly. Surely after a whole month she would miss Rory terribly and be only too glad to rush home and fall into his arms!

When Angela came indoors, she was feeling so excited that she couldn't help telling Nancy that very moment.

The younger girl listened to her sister's enthusiastic plans critically. Nancy resembled Angela, except that her hair was more of a honey-blond and her eyes were gray-blue and reflective.

"Are you actually going to leave Rory here alone?" Nancy asked, incredulous. "That's a crazy thing to do, just to see your silly old friend."

Angela, her enthusiasm momentarily dampened, looked at Nancy with wonderment. Nancy was two years younger than Angela but had always seemed older in some ways. She never had a single frivolous notion. Sober and practical, that was Nancy. She had taken a business degree at college and had already begun to work in Rory's law office for the summer.

"But Nancy," Angela said, almost pleadingly, "it will only be for a month. I asked Rory to come with me—"

"Of course he can't," exclaimed Nancy heatedly. "He had the Simmons case coming up the second week in July."

Angela felt abashed. Nancy knew more about Rory's work than she did.

"Is Rory going to let you go, just like that?" Nancy asked.

"Well, yes," admitted Angela. "He knows how much I'd like to see Stephanie." Some instinct prevented Angela from confiding that Rory expected them to get married when she returned. Angela had a nagging feeling that Rory should have minded more that she would be away. Not that he had any reason to be jealous, she quickly assured herself. Still, if he

10

loved her, he ought to be just a little bit more upset than he was. And yet, would she not bitterly resent it if he prevented her from going?

Another letter arrived from Stephanie the following day, and Angela opened it with trembling fingers. She was afraid that Stephanie might have changed her mind. In fact, her friend had written again in order to impart some exciting news.

I'm engaged! It's official! Niko and I will be married in October! Perhaps you and Rory can come to Athens and make it a double wedding. Oh, wait until you meet Niko! He is absolutely gorgeous, completely the opposite of me, and we fight like cats and dogs, but we always make it up with tears and kisses. Niko is so jealous he looks daggers at anybody I speak to. . . .

As she read her friend's letter Angela grew envious. It was clear that Stephanie adored her Niko, that she had not a single doubt about their marriage. If only Angela could feel the same about Rory!

The next few days were hectic and flew by so quickly that before Angela could properly digest what was happening she was at the airport and Rory was saying good-bye to her. "Have a good time, Angie, and don't forget to write," he said, kissing her gently.

For a moment Angela had a qualm. He seemed so self-possessed, so reasonable. Angela tried to convince herself that his behavior proved that he loved her. He wanted her to be happy, so he was encouraging her to have her little trip. And yet, why did she feel let down? Why did she want him to grab her and pull her into his arms, kiss her with abandon, murmur that he loved her and would be counting the days? But that was not Rory's way, and never had been. He never went overboard about anything—and that included Angela.

"Won't you—won't you miss me a little?" Angela ventured tremulously.

"Of course I'll miss you, but it's you who chose to go, remember."

Angela felt fearful. Oh, he was reasonable, she couldn't blame him, and yet . . . and yet . . . She kissed him with some abandon to make up for her confused feelings, but he remained undemonstrative as always.

Angela was vastly relieved when her plane took off, soaring into the pale blue sky and lifting her spirits with it. She was truly on her way to Greece!

Stephanie had taught Angela many Greek words, but she now studied her Greek phrase book to refresh her memory.

When the plane touched down in Paris, Angela went for a brief walk around the air terminal, excited to be in Paris even if she would see no more of it than the elegant airport tourist shops. On impulse she bought a silk scarf for Stephanie.

Returning to the plane, Angela saw that she now had a neighbor, a good-looking, dark young man who took one glance at her and jumped to his feet.

"It is your first visit to Greece?" he asked in slightly foreign English.

"Yes," Angela answered, painfully shy as usual when talking to strangers.

The young man was frankly staring at her with lively, mischievous dark eyes—eyes that reminded her of Stephanie's, for of course he was Greek himself. Of medium height, and rather slight in build, he wore a red turtleneck shirt that set off his dark, wavy hair and rosy complexion.

12

"You are the most beautiful girl I have ever seen," he announced in a matter-of-fact way, "and we are going to be best friends until I am finished with my studies in Paris. Then, of course, we will be married."

Angela laughed. "As simple as that?"

"Why not? A Greek sees what he wants and makes sure to get it. Unless you're already married," he amended mischievously, his quick eyes having noticed that she wore no ring. Angela had left her diamond at home, telling Nancy that it would be safer.

Now Angela started guiltily. "I—I'm already engaged," she confessed, flushing.

"So what? You'll break it off and marry me because you won't find anybody better. What's your name?"

His curiosity was insatiable. He went on to ask her age, education, family background, her purpose in coming to Greece. Seeing the slightly shocked expression on Angela's face, the boy laughed merrily. "We Greeks ask what is on our minds and say what is in our hearts. It is better so. Anyway, my name is Savvas. I'm studying at the university in Paris, even though I am already twenty-five." He shrugged. "I have spent my youth enjoying myself. And I am very rich, so I will be able to give you everything. Meantime, here is a kiss." Savvas leaned over quickly and brushed her cheek with his warm lips.

Angela felt a delicious shiver down her spine, although her face flooded with embarrassment. Several times he took her hand in his own, making her acutely aware of his attractiveness.

The time passed so quickly that Angela was surprised when Savvas looked at his watch and noted that they would soon be landing in Athens. "I have been doing all the talking. Tell me, what is the name of your girl friend in Athens?"

"Stephanie," Angela murmured.

Savvas rolled his eyes upward. "Stephanie! But that is the name of every Greek girl not called Maria. Stephanie who?"

"Pallas," Angela said reluctantly.

"Pallas? The publishing family?" His unruly eyebrows arched, and he stared at her, suddenly subdued.

"Why, yes. But how did you know?"

"My little Angela, I know everything. The Pallas family is very important. Oh, yes, I know the name Pallas." He smiled suddenly, showing small, even teeth. "It is as I said. We will see much of each other. I, too, am important in Athens."

"Are all your countrymen as modest as you are?" Angela asked Savvas with a smile. She was beginning to feel at ease with this preposterous young man.

"Of course I am not modest. 'If you don't sing the praise of your own house,' goes an old Greek proverb, 'it will fall down on your head.'"

"From that calamity your head is perfectly safe, though it seems swollen for quite another reason."

Savvas laughed appreciatively. "You have a quick tongue, that is good. A woman should have a little vinegar on her lips to cut the sweetness of the honey. Pah, put away that silly book. I will teach you all the Greek you need to know." Savvas insisted upon giving her a lesson until the plane touched down in Athens.

Angela waited near the luggage counter for her bags, while Savvas, at her side, looked about him restlessly. "Just now I'm in a terrific hurry. But don't worry, Angelamou, we will meet again." He gave her a hug and in a moment he was gone.

Angela felt a little let down, even though she had not taken Savvas seriously. Wasn't he too typically Greek, she thought wryly, remembering Stephanie's flights of fancy, which were rarely followed through.

"Angela! Angela!" Stephanie's voice rang out from the crowd waiting at the arrival gate.

Angela waved back enthusiastically. It was the Stephanie she remembered: her dark hair, as shiny as patent leather, falling sleekly below her ears, her round face happily alight with a broad smile.

As Angela slowly edged forward behind other passengers she noticed that Stephanie was speaking to a man standing slightly behind her. Angela felt a fluttering sensation in her stomach. He had the sort of proud bearing and impressive dark looks that marked him as someone of leadership and prominence. Also he seemed familiar.

He stood taller than most Greeks and was dressed in a cream-colored suit set off by a cornflower-blue shirt open at the collar. His face, above a strong neck, was not exactly handsome, but Angela couldn't take her eyes off him. His rugged oval face was heightened by high cheekbones and straight brows that joined over a high-bridged Grecian nose. The mouth beneath was firm, with a sensual cut to the lips. They looked capable of decisiveness and surely passion. Angela blushed at the thought, her eyes quickly moving to his hair, which was black and thick, falling in glossy waves.

This was undoubtedly Stephanie's fiancé. A sudden stab of envy went through Angela, causing her to feel thoroughly ashamed. Angela Blair, get a grip on yourself, she told herself sternly. Stephanie was her best friend, and if she had had the good fortune to attract the love of such a man as this, good for her. No wonder Stephanie had written of him with such enthusiasm. But where had Angela seen him before?

There was no time for further speculation, for Stephanie flung her arms around Angela, kissed her on both cheeks, and sent forth an impetuous stream of

15

words that immediately put Angela's head into a whirl. Typically, Stephanie neglected to introduce her companion.

She let go of Angela finally and nudged him. "I said she was gorgeous. Was I right?"

"Just this once, yes." His low-pitched, vibrant voice sent a strange thrill through Angela, while his black, luminous eyes seared her with their intensity. "I can understand the attraction between you. Snow White and Rose Red." He spoke perfect English with no trace of a Greek accent.

Then he extended his hand coolly without smiling. *"Kalós írthate.* Welcome to Greece, Angela Blair." His strong, warm hand burned her cold and trembling fingers.

"Kalós sas uríkame," Angela replied shyly, hoping her pronunciation wasn't too ludicrous.

"Oh, isn't she marvelous!" exclaimed Stephanie, kissing Angela again.

Her companion, letting his mouth curl into a slightly mocking smile, merely picked up Angela's bags and led the way to the car.

When they reached the large black Mercedes Stephanie broke her chatter to exclaim, "Let me drive, Alex, do. I want to show off for Angela."

"Certainly not. What would anyone think, seeing you drive while I am sitting in the car, except that I lack arms, wits, or both."

Pouting, Stephanie bade Angela slide in next to the driver, while she took her seat near the window.

Alex? Angela probed her memory. This must be Stephanie's brother! Her older brother, who had been educated in England. He had married against the wishes of his family, and there had been some scandal about his wife, but Angela couldn't remember what it was. She knew only that the wife had died and left two

16

children. It was this niece and nephew to whom Angela was supposed to teach English.

As the sleek car took them from the airport along a main road flanked with low stucco buildings, Stephanie kept up a running conversation.

"Our parents are already on the island, so it's just us three, and Alex's children, of course, and the servants. Wait until you see our house on the hill, Lycabettus, which rises up in the middle of the city, like a volcano from nowhere. . . ."

Although Angela kept her eyes straight ahead, she was extremely conscious of Alex next to her. He had put on sunglasses, which gave him a somewhat sinister appearance.

The mysterious Alex had intrigued Angela five years before when Stephanie had first mentioned him and told her his story. Angela had imagined Alex as a tragic Greek hero in the grip of fate. Now she felt he was master not only of his own fate but of everyone else's.

As Angela stole a sideways glance at him his perfect Grecian profile suddenly revealed why he seemed so familiar. Alex resembled a bronze statue of Apollo. Angela had often stared at the color photograph in one of the glossy Pallas art books given her by Stephanie. Apollo was the god of the Sun, music, and poetry. Angela didn't know about the music and poetry, but from what she had so far seen of Alex Pallas, she could almost believe that the sun came up and went down at his bidding.

She was aware of his strong hand moving from the wheel to the floor shift beside her, of his thigh disturbingly close to her own. Angela was having difficulty with her breathing, and she didn't dare examine why she felt so relieved that this man at her side was not Stephanie's Niko after all.

17

As they approached the center of Athens Angela's attention was caught by the gleaming white buildings, dazzling under the sun's glare. They tended to be fairly low, for it was a law that nothing should obstruct the view of the Acropolis, and marble had been used lavishly in their construction. Everything looked so gay. Almost every building boasted a series of deep balconies, hung with bright blue awnings, while the windows had varnished wooden shutters. The city's shops were beginning to close for the long siesta.

"After the concert tonight at the Herodes Atticus theater at the foot of the Acropolis, we'll have dinner in Plaka. . . ."

Angela was torn between listening to Stephanie and forming her own impressions of Athens.

As if he had read her mind, Alex said, "Be quiet now, Stephanie, and let your friend get her bearings."

"Yes, you're right. Excuse me, Angela. I'm just so excited to see you." Stephanie switched to Greek and directed her conversation to her brother.

The car climbed the very steep, tree-lined Lycabettus Hill and finally drove through a richly ornamented gate along a gravel driveway bordered with stately Italian cypresses. They halted in front of a huge yellow nineteenth-century mansion with a pair of flower-laden magnolias at both sides of the entrance.

Inside, it was dark and cool behind the closed shutters, and Angela had a fleeting awareness of high ceilings, heavy tapestries, and opulent furnishings.

She was glad to be alone for a few minutes in her large room, which contained a canopied four-poster, the sort of bed she had seen only in museums.

After washing, Angela put on a pale blue thin dress that set off her slim figure and left her arms bare and cool. She was just brushing her long hair when she heard a knock on her door.

18

"Steph, is that you?"

There was a pause. Then a male voice said, "Come, Angela, I will take you down to lunch."

Angela was puzzled. It didn't sound at all like Alex. When she opened the door she found Savvas! He stood there smiling impudently and then squeezed her arm with bold familiarity. "I told you we would meet again, Angelamou, though you hardly thought so soon.'"

"But—but what are you doing here?" she asked foolishly.

"I live here. I am Savvas Pallas, the second brother," he finished, making her a sweeping, exaggerated bow.

Of course! Angela had completely forgotten that Stephanie had two brothers. "I came on ahead so as not to spoil your welcome by sharing it," Savvas told her as they came down the majestic staircase. "We Greeks don't always push ourselves forward," he rebuked her gently.

Angela smiled happily at him. Now his resemblance to Stephanie seemed even more marked, not only in looks but in good humor and high spirits.

Quite a commotion followed in the dining room. Stephanie and a small boy and girl surrounded Savvas, the children jumping on their uncle like puppies. All of them shouted so much that they set the magnificent crystal chandelier in tinkling motion.

Angela, who tended to adore all children, took an immediate liking to six-year-old Miki and his sister, Crista, a year younger. With their jet-black curls and shiny eyes like black buttons, set in round, red-cheeked faces, they looked very much like their aunt and uncle. Certainly they had none of their father's reserve.

"I'm afraid they hardly know any English," Stephanie explained to Angela, who was saying a few simple

19

words to Miki, while Crista hid her face in her hands. Angela then tried out her elementary Greek.

Savvas exploded with pride. "Bravo, Angela. She is like a sponge with our language," he told Stephanie. "I myself taught her on the plane." He explained how they had met, while the servants carried plates from the kitchen.

"All right now, children, that will do," said a voice with calm authority.

Angela felt her pulse suddenly quicken as Alex took his seat at the head of the table. He spoke firmly to his children in Greek, and they immediately became subdued.

Angela was puzzled at her inability to control the odd way her heart beat and her breath grew short every time she looked at Alex Pallas. The very sound of his voice sent shivery waves rippling through her.

As they ate, Angela confined her conversation to yes and no. She felt uncomfortable, and was made even more timid by Savvas's constant attentions to her. He was explaining each Greek dish with care, adding to her confusion. And through it all, whenever she glanced at Alex, she caught his eye. The brooding look he bestowed upon her set her heart to pounding so strongly that she feared it would be heard above the din.

Angela didn't wish to look at Alex, but her eye strayed to the head of the table again and again. There was something electrifying about him, and it seemed to catch her up in its spell. Angela began to wonder what had happened to his wife, and why he had never remarried.

"Come, Angela," Savvas requested, pushing back her chair and offering her his arm. "We go to your room and have a siesta now."

Angela's cheeks turned crimson, but immediately

20

she realized she had misunderstood. Savvas was intending only to lead her to her door, not go inside with her!

"I—I never sleep in the afternoon," Angela objected softly, while Savvas snorted.

"You must, little one, or you will be tired tonight, for we stay up to all hours."

"My brother is right," Alex said in his low, thrilling voice. "You may at first find our ways different, but I trust you will be able to accommodate yourself quickly." He granted her a rather mocking smile that made her catch her breath in confusion.

"I'll wake you in time to dress for dinner," Stephanie promised as Savvas led Angela away.

She did believe Savvas would have pushed his way into her room if she had hesitated for a moment. Fortunately she had the presence to shut the door quickly behind her. Then Angela went to the window and threw open her shutters. There, in the distance, was the Acropolis, the glittering sun on the ruined pillars of the ancient temple making it seem covered with jewels.

Suddenly Angela felt very happy. She sank into the soft pillows on her bed and realized that she was tired after all. In no time she had fallen asleep. She dreamed of hills, ruins, and ancient glories, while the Sun god, Apollo, floated weightlessly over her head, smiling sardonically at her like Alex Pallas.

Chapter Two

When Angela awoke, she found Stephanie sitting beside her bed. "I have been watching you dream. It must have been pleasant because you were smiling in your sleep. You dreamed of Rory, eh?"

Without replying, Angela swung her legs over the bed, her cheeks flushing.

Stephanie showed her the bathroom, and Angela stepped into the shower, letting the stream of cool water wash away her drowsiness.

While Angela dressed, Stephanie remained in her room, chatting animatedly about her fiancé. "Niko came to my birthday party last year, when he first began to work for Alex, who is at the head of everything since Papa retired. Niko is Alex's right-hand man, so practical, so good at supervising and coordinating the various companies. Anyway, my parents had already drawn up the marriage contract—don't look so horrified. They wouldn't have forced me to marry Niko if I hadn't wanted it. Alex, in fact, hates arranged marriages. Of course, I fell in love with Niko that very first evening. And so will you. He was born in Crete. They are a race apart, the Cretans, proud and suspicious. If Niko gets an idea into his head nothing can dislodge it. Still, his firmness makes up for my own deficiencies. Look, I'll draw you a picture of him."

Angela smiled. This was the same Stephanie who,

when her English failed her, used to resort to pencil and paper. She was, in fact, a very good artist and was now doing book illustrations for the children's department at Pallas Publishing.

With a few deft strokes Stephanie sketched a curly-headed fellow, broad-shouldered, with a scowling face that made him look downright villainous. Stephanie, thought Angela, probably smiled enough for both of them.

Stephanie watched with admiration as Angela put on an Indian-print silk dress, its muted blues and reds setting off her shoulder-length golden hair and violet-blue eyes. "You look stunning. Better stay very close to us this evening or you'll be kidnapped for sure."

When Savvas joined the girls downstairs, he kissed Angela's hand and went into such raptures over her appearance that she became acutely embarrassed. Rory had never paid her extravagant compliments, and she was most unaccustomed to such attention.

The three had an exciting ride in a cable car to the top of Lycabettus and found seats at a table in the small café. While Savvas ordered drinks, Angela and Stephanie watched the Sun go down. The great globe of orange deepened in color as if burning itself out, finally dipping from view, leaving a deep blue sky slashed with purple. The city below them took on a muted, pastel quality that Angela found breathtaking.

"This is ouzo," announced Savvas, pouring a colorless liquid into Angela's glass. "Now, watch." As he added ice and water the drink turned milky. He laughed proudly as if he had performed a magic trick, and Angela found his merriment contagious.

"Now try some *mezedákia*, little hors d'oeuvres. A Greek never drinks without eating."

The waiter had set down a platter·containing stuffed vine leaves, black and green olives, and bite-size pieces of strong cheese. Savvas insisted on feeding Angela little morsels himself, demanding to know if they weren't wonderful. While she laughingly agreed, there was something nagging at her, and she finally identified it as the absence of Alex. Surely Stephanie had said he would be joining them for dinner. Without being aware of it, Angela kept turning her head toward the entrance to the *tavérna*.

"Don't worry, Alex will be here," said the observant Savvas. His perception caused Angela to redden. How she deplored her inability to control her blushing.

"Never mind Alex. I am here now." Savvas leaned forward and stroked Angela's bare arm lightly with his fingertip.

"Let her alone, for goodness sake, Savvas. She's not a Parisian student on the Boul' Mich to be flirted with so outrageously. Besides, she's already engaged to Rory Martin, tall, blond, and very handsome. They make a perfect couple," Stephanie assured her brother.

Angela felt her face grow hotter. She was unreasonably irritated at the mention of Rory and hated herself for her treachery. Stephanie had every right to bring Rory into the conversation. He was supposed to be Angela's fiancé, after all.

"But this Rory is across the ocean, and I am here," Savvas replied with impeccable logic, smiling impishly. "Tonight Angela is with me, as you will have Niko, and Alex will have Petra."

"Who is Petra?" Startled, Angela had asked the question sharply before having time to check herself.

"Petra Leonidas, the girl Alex was supposed to marry but didn't, and thereby hangs a tale—"

"Savvas! That's enough!" Stephanie's eyes flashed at her brother in disapproval.

"You must never talk to *me* like that, my little Stephanie," said a new voice behind them.

24

"Oh, Niko, how you startled me." Stephanie jumped up and embraced him. "Let me present my American sister, Angela Blair. This is the famous Niko Goudelis.'"

Niko kissed Angela on both cheeks in the Greek manner, stepping back to regard her with pleasure. "Welcome, Angela. I have heard much about you from Stephanie. Even so, your beauty is unexpected." He continued to stare at her through long, narrow, rather hooded dark eyes.

"I've heard about you, too. You—you look like the drawing Stephanie did of you," Angela replied quickly, trying to overcome her shyness. Niko did resemble his portrait, right down to the scowl. He was of medium height, very broad-shouldered and sturdy, his blue-black hair falling in glossy curls all around his head. He was a shade darker than any of the others, and his features were hawklike. Especially disturbing were the eyes, like watermelon seeds. Angela had never been scrutinized with such open curiosity as by these Greeks, and she found it difficult to become accustomed to it.

To her relief Niko turned his gaze to Savvas. "So, the prodigal son returns, eh? What is it, kicked out of university for flirting with the girls?"

"Never mind your jokes, Niko. Just concern yourself with my sister and let me pay homage to the beautiful Angela."

Niko, who spoke English less fluently than the others, and with a stronger accent, switched to Greek. The two men began to talk loudly, with gestures.

"That will do, Savvas," said a thrilling voice at Angela's elbow. She spun around, flustered, to see Alex smiling mockingly, his eyes upon her. "At least make a pretense of good manners to show our guest that modern Greeks are not the barbarians they sometimes seem."

25

Angela found that she was short of breath, and her discomfort wasn't helped when she was introduced to Alex's companion, Petra Leonidas, who now came forward from the shadows.

Angela felt as if her heart would burst right through the thin material of her dress. Petra was beautiful. She was taller and heavier than Angela, and perhaps two or three years older. Petra's magnificent black hair cascaded almost to her waist, and she wore a dress of shimmering taffeta, the color of blood, the neckline plunging so that her full bosom was partly revealed. Encircling her throat was a choker of heavy spun gold in the shape of a snake—a replica of an ancient necklace, Angela surmised. Her arms jingled with gold bracelets, some repeating the snake motif, as did a gold ring on her finger. Petra's eyes were a deep, startling blue, and as icy as a frozen pond. She scarcely condescended to look at Angela after being introduced, gazing past her as if she were of no significance.

Petra certainly seemed haughty, but still, with such beauty, why had Alex originally refused to marry her? The vague details that Angela could recall from Stephanie's account so long ago had faded. What had stuck in her mind was an impression that Alex's intended had been unattractive. How wrong Angela had been was now disturbingly apparent to her. Equally obvious was that Alex was now paying court to Petra.

"The concert begins at seven exactly. Hadn't we better leave?" Petra turned to Alex, her rich contralto giving an added importance to what she said.

For a moment Alex's gaze rested on Angela broodingly. Then he focused on Petra, granting her a brilliant smile.

Angela suddenly felt heavyhearted. She sat silently in the back of the Mercedes during their journey, staring at the back of Alex's head as he drove, noticing the way his heavy hair curled down over the collar of his cream-colored jacket. Petra nestled close to him, speaking softly for his ears alone.

When Angela found herself in the ancient amphitheater of Herodes Atticus, a rising excitement dispelled her sadness. Their seats were the original stone steps, covered with flat cushions, and every seat was filled. At the rear of the stage stood the ruins of an ancient structure serving as a dramatic backdrop.

The orchestra members took their places. When the conductor raised his baton, the audience grew silent. The sounds of Beethoven's *Egmont* overture filled the air. Angela's eyes followed the opening notes into the navy-blue sky, alight with more stars than she could remember ever having seen at one time.

Listening to the music, Angela felt an exhilaration, an awareness of historic continuity. Spectators had sat in these very seats almost two thousand years ago under the same stars that seemed to lift one closer to the heavens.

Angela scarcely noticed that Alex sat with his arm around Petra, nor did she feel Savvas's insistent hand closing over her own. She was totally entranced by her surroundings and by the beautiful sounds surely meant for the gods. Just as the music reached a crescendo during the final number, Wagner's overture to Tannhaüser—with horns blaring, drums beating, cymbals clashing—an enormous moon rose over the craggy backdrop to lend its majesty to the swelling final notes.

Angela remained mute with awe until the thundering applause brought her back to the present, and the reality that the concert had ended.

In Plaka the bright lights and insistent beat of a different kind of music cast its own spell. Guided by Savvas, his hand firmly on her arm, Angela strolled up

27

the winding streets and staircases of this old town huddled around the foot of the Acropolis. People still lived in the aging stucco dwellings with wooden upper stories, red-tiled roofs, and flower-filled courtyards.

Angela wondered how the residents slept. All along the step-covered streets was an unbroken series of *tavernas*, nearly all boasting their own little bands, dominated by the mandolin-shaped bouzouki. Scattered on the broad steps were people eating and drinking at tables and clapping their hands to the insistent rhythms. There were also young men dancing, their hands raised over twirling handkerchiefs.

Alex led their party to a restaurant on a raised terrace flanked with bamboo trellises entwined with grapevines. There, seated at a large round table with a white cloth and napkins—which marked the restaurant as superior to the others—they ate their meal and drank retsina. Angela hoped she would grow to like the Greek resinated wine more than she did at first taste.

So much was going on at once that Angela felt as if she were at a three-ring circus. There was an array of strange dishes in front of her, and she grew flustered when the only things she could positively identify were roast meat, potatoes, and salad. At that point Savvas devoted himself totally to her, not only describing each Greek dish but telling her the word for it.

Angela tried to pay attention to what Savvas was saying, but she found it difficult. Her glance kept straying to Petra, sitting directly across the table and snuggling so close to Alex that she was practically in his lap. Taking bits of food on her fork, Petra teased Alex with them, making him reach. Each time his eyes met Angela's they narrowed in mockery, causing her to look away in confusion. Petra continued to ignore Angela, while Stephanie sought to speak to her in shouted bursts. Niko requested different tunes from the orchestra and threw hundred-drachma notes at their feet until the floor near the trio was carpeted with money.

Angela had never been assailed by such conflicting emotions. She was excited by her surroundings, by the compelling and, she thought, highly romantic music. Certainly she could not remember a scene of such uninhibited gaiety. At the same time, the presence of Alex and Petra dampened her euphoria, and she scolded herself silently for allowing them to disturb her composure.

It seemed to her that they lingered at the table for hours, nibbling fruit and an exquisite creamy white cheese called *manoúri,* washing it down with wine.

Intercepting an intimate glance between Alex and Petra, Angela suddenly felt exhausted, and once more sadness overcame her. It was envy, she was thinking, envy of the two couples seated at the table, behaving so differently from the way she and Rory did together.

Angela sternly bid herself to cease being so maudlin or she would begin to cry. Undoubtedly the unfamiliar exotic spices and wine were having a strange effect upon her, causing her face to burn and her eyes to smart.

Excusing herself, she got up from the table and stepped outside the restaurant. She wanted to wash her burning face but had no idea of where to do so. Perhaps if she simply moved away from the heat of the lights, the smoke, and the loud music, she would feel cooler in the fresh breeze.

She saw with dismay, however, that she didn't dare wander far. The crowds were thick and boisterous, and there was a danger of being pushed and pulled along with them. She would never find her way back to the Pallas party in this maze of winding streets, so she merely moved down the first side street, a narrow

29

alley, and stood in the entrance of a courtyard, breathing in the soothing aroma of roses that grew down over the wooden gate.

Angela jumped in fright as a young Greek, walking past, stopped and began to talk to her rapidly. He was darkly handsome, in tight trousers and a shirt unbuttoned to the navel.

Angela backed away, shaking her head. "No, no, I don't understand."

The man, smiling at her timidity, came closer. He took a handful of her golden hair and crooned over it.

Abruptly he was knocked off-balance from behind.

Angela blushed furiously when she saw that it was Alex Pallas who had come to her rescue.

After he spoke some angry words in Greek to the man, who made an apologetic gesture and hastened away, Alex turned to Angela.

"You are never to go anywhere at night by yourself," he said in a commanding tone. "You will always see to it that I or Savvas or Niko are with you, Miss Blair. It is the same for my sister."

Angela felt mortified to be given orders in this fashion. "I'm not accustomed to being told what to do as if I were a child," she informed him sullenly. "I can take care of myself."

"Yes, I noticed how well you can do so," Alex retorted, curling his lip.

"I was handling the situation. He would have gone away—"

"No doubt holding you by the hair. My dear young lady, don't presume to tell me about my own countrymen. You will simply obey my instructions in future."

"Really!" Angela cried, an unaccustomed feeling of injury compelling her stubbornly to contradict him. "I'm used to being independent—"

"Of course. Independence," Alex said scornfully. "I

know all about American female independence. I am no stranger to your country. I make business trips to all the major cities quite often. The men treat their women very casually. A woman is free to walk down any street in a provocative manner—"

"That's not true," Angela countered hotly. "Provocation is in the eye of the beholder. At least women are free to walk down the street, period. Here, I suppose, you prefer to lock them in the house." Angela didn't know where she found the courage to speak this way to Alex Pallas. She had never talked so angrily to anyone before. Perhaps it was the wine. . . .

"You have drunk too much wine," Alex observed derisively, reading her mind with infuriating accuracy, "or you wouldn't say such silly things."

"I have not drunk too much wine," she retorted defiantly, but immediately shrank before him. His eyes scorched her with such intensity that Angela suddenly felt striped of her defenses.

"You illustrate my point exactly," he continued, as his gaze traveled impersonally from her face to her neck, her bosom, and down to her slender, well-shaped legs. "Look at you. Your flowing hair, that clinging dress, the languorous way you walk. . . ." Alex smiled sardonically.

Angela caught her breath and began to tremble, while she felt the back of her neck and her ears burn hotly with humiliation. Tears began to cloud her eyes, and she was unable to utter a sound for fear that she might cry out of frustration and embarrassment.

Alex knew very well that he was making her miserable, but he seemed determined to drive his point home. It was clear that he had no liking for "independent" women, and least of all for her.

"My sister tells me you are engaged to be married," he continued in his mocking tone, "and yet here you

31

are alone. No doubt he encouraged you, told you to have fun—"

"That—that isn't so," Angela interrupted, furious at the uncanny way Alex had put his finger on the truth.

"I do not propose to stand here in the street and argue with you, Miss Blair," Alex announced with arrogant finality. "You are a guest in my country and in my house. I am responsible for you."

"I can easily cease to be your guest," Angela countered, and immediately regretted her words. How childish they sounded.

"That is entirely up to you. However, we will return to the table now."

He whirled and stalked down the street. Angela, feeling foolish and still dangerously close to tears, trailed in his wake.

When she slipped into her seat at the table, she felt even more flushed and uncomfortable than before.

Petra's cold blue eyes flickered over her insolently. "My dear, if you went to make some repairs to your face, it was a wasted trip. The nose is still shiny, and you forgot the lipstick."

Mortified, Angela longed to point out that she wore hardly any makeup, whereas Petra was painted heavily enough to go in front of the footlights. However, she deplored the sort of catfight that Petra seemed capable of provoking, so she kept her silence.

Savvas, who had been talking to Stephanie and Niko in Greek, now resumed his attentions to Angela, but for her the evening was quite spoiled.

As Alex dropped Petra at her door Angela watched surreptitiously through the window as he kissed her good night. The sight only increased her despondency.

When Alex returned to the car, he noted that the other four were in the backseat. His eye flicking impersonally over Angela, Alex said abruptly, "Savvas, come up front. We have to talk."

"Business, always business," said Stephanie, yawning. She put her head on Niko's shoulder and went to sleep. Angela, sitting on Niko's other side, was sleepy herself. She was half-dozing when she felt an arm steal around her shoulders and move down to her waist, the fingers lightly stroking her bare arm.

Angela opened her eyes in astonishment. She could dimly see that Niko was glaring at her with loathing, but he would not relax his grip. Angela began to grow alarmed. She couldn't free herself, nor could she say anything.

As they drove through a dark stretch Niko abruptly leaned over and kissed her lips.

"Don't!" she whispered fiercely, pulling her head away.

Savvas turned and tried to see into the rear of the car. "What's going on there?"

"Nothing," Niko answered in a cold voice. "The girls have been kept up too late. Both are asleep now." He switched to Greek.

Angela guessed from his altered tone that he had changed the subject. She felt absolutely wretched. What kind of game was he playing? Why was he treating her this way? Didn't he fear that she would tell Stephanie about his behavior? She fully intended to do so the first thing in the morning.

Angela began to feel that she had blundered into a very complex situation. Her relationship with Stephanie had always been so warm and open, but that had been in her own home territory. Now she was in a foreign place, and apparently did not in the least understand the customs of her hosts. She must have done something wrong to have made Niko so hostile toward her. When they had first been introduced, he had been

33

perfectly polite, even admiring. Why had he changed toward her? She now remembered that he had given her some angry glances at the dinner table. Was it because of Savvas and his playful attentions? Or was it after she had returned with Alex?

Angela recalled the way Stephanie and Niko had been looking at each other earlier. It had seemed obvious that they were very much in love. Then why was Niko annoying Angela so rudely and risking his engagement? What puzzled her most was that he had forced his embraces upon her even though he apparently disapproved of her.

Angela was vastly relieved when Alex dropped Niko off. Stephanie drowsily embraced him and transferred her head to Angela's shoulder. Niko gave Angela a parting glare that added to her apprehensions.

When they arrived home, Savvas began to grumble because Stephanie was so deeply asleep that he had to carry her into the house while Alex parked the car.

Angela groped her way into the kitchen for a drink of water. The food and wine had made her terribly thirsty.

So exhausted that she could barely climb the stairs, Angela did so slowly and halted when she reached the top. On both sides of the hall were a number of closed doors. Angela couldn't remember which was hers. She stood still for a moment, feeling very foolish.

A door opened and shut, and Savvas came toward her. "Eh, Angela, you are waiting for me to escort you to your room. That is the way you must always behave." As he encircled her waist and led her to her room, she noted its position carefully. "Thank you, Savvas. It's been a lovely evening. Good night." She put her hand on the doorknob, only to feel Savvas place his warm hand over hers.

"And my reward?" He turned her gently, his hands

34

moving to her shoulders, caressing them lightly. "Don't you know it is impolite to say good night to a Greek without a kiss?"

Gingerly he kissed her left, then her right cheek. Suddenly his mouth sought her lips.

Angela twisted her head. "You said a kiss. You've already had two."

"Pah, those kisses are as unfriendly as a handshake. And I am feeling particularly friendly to you, my little Angela." He pressed his mouth against hers, holding her shoulders insistently to keep her from breaking away.

After an initial resistance, Angela ceased to struggle. She was simply too weary, so she shut her eyes and lost herself in the sweetness of the moment. She was aware that the hall was spinning slightly, and she felt somewhat faint.

There was an impatient movement behind them, and Angela nearly toppled over as Savvas abruptly released her.

It was Alex. He hissed something at his brother. For a moment Savvas glared back and seemed on the verge of defiance, but the instant passed and he stomped to his room.

"I must apologize for my brother, Miss Blair," Alex said sullenly. "His manners are not always what one might desire."

Flushing darkly, Angela detected an ironic note, as if Alex were deliberately shifting all the blame to Savvas although he knew very well that she had permitted the embrace.

Quickly meeting his penetrating gaze, Angela had to drop her eyes.

"Savvas, I fear, is still a child in many ways." And so are you, Alex implied.

Angela felt the blood leave her face, and a momentary panic overtook her as the vertigo increased. She leaned her head against the doorjamb, hoping she would not disgrace herself even further by passing out at Alex's feet.

"What is it, Miss Blair? Are you all right?"

"Just slightly dizzy. It will go away in a moment."

Alex drew closer, a look of concern replacing the mockery in his eyes. He took her arm and supported her firmly while he opened her door and switched on the light.

His touch made her flesh tingle, but it helped her dizziness.

"I'm all right now. Really. Thank you."

"I'll say good night then, Miss Blair."

"Good night, Mr. Pallas," she murmured.

"Kalinikhta," he repeated huskily, his face so close to hers that she could feel his warm breath on her aching forehead. She feared for an instant that he would kiss her, and then was angry with herself for being disappointed when he did not. He simply turned and withdrew down the hall.

What was wrong with her? Was it the air, the wine, the utter strangeness of everything that had so disoriented her? She had never behaved this way in her life, nor had she suffered from such disturbing thoughts.

Certainly she had drunk too much wine. When she lay down in bed, the room swam, and her thoughts swam with it, as mingled as colors in a kaleidoscope.

Every encounter with Alex Pallas left her shaken. His cool arrogance and mockery were bad enough, but the concerned manner in which he had taken her arm and led her into her room had unnerved her even further because it had been so unexpected. What was it about this enigmatic man that altered her breathing, her heartbeat, the very texture of her skin? Angela had never experienced anything like this before, and she was frightened. If she had not known better, she could almost have believed she had been drugged. Certainly she was not used to being touched so unceremoniously the way the Greeks touched her. Each time it happened she was so stunned that she waited too long to react as firmly as she should.

Angela tossed restlessly, only worsening her dizziness. She was sorely tempted to pack her bags and take the next plane home. Was it possible that only yesterday she had been safe in Springport, her life orderly and predictable, her respiration normal?

She shut her eyes tightly and tried to forget Savvas, Niko, and especially Alex, by thinking of Rory. Desperately she tried to summon up his face—and couldn't. In place of his frank blue eyes she saw dark brown ones—mischievous, glowering, angry, passionate. Panic seized her. It was only a day since she'd parted from Rory and already his features had faded from her memory. If only he would write and summon her. If only it were a desperate letter, full of longing for her, of words of love. Then she remembered the letters he had written in the past. They had been nononsense communications, not the sort of letters she had wanted to tie with pink ribbon and hide in the attic. She doubted that it would ever occur to Rory to write that sort of letter.

A dim gray light was filtering through the shutters when Angela finally fell asleep—only to dream that she was lost in Plaka, wandering up and down the steps, the old houses leaning crazily toward her, trying to crush her. On every side she was assailed by bouzouki players who tried to attract her attention. Then she came face to face with Rory. She tried to call his name but no sound came, and he passed her by with no sign of recognition.

Chapter Three

Angela could barely remember her troubles in the morning because, upon opening the shutters, she saw that the day was beautiful—a cloudless sky and a bright Sun beaming its golden rays on the entire city. She gazed at the Acropolis with a heightened sense of excitement. Surely she couldn't think of leaving Greece just because of a silly misunderstanding.

When Angela entered the large, cool dining room, where the sun slanted through the partly closed shutters onto the heavy oak table, she found herself in the midst of a domestic commotion.

Crista and Miki were sitting at the table alone, sulking, while Maria, the maid, shouted at them to eat their breakfast. It was clear to Angela that they were refusing to do so.

Angela smiled at them and said good morning. "How are you?" she asked carefully.

Miki glowered and made her a long complaint in Greek. "I don't understand. I don't speak Greek," Angela replied in Greek.

"I don't speak English," countered Crista in English, giggling.

Angela laughed with her at the absurdity of both statements, and even Miki allowed himself a grin. "I know what we'll do," said Angela. "I'll teach you English, and you'll teach me Greek."

Maria brought her fresh rolls, steaming coffee, and a boiled egg.

Angela had never been shy with children, and for the first time since arriving in Athens she felt completely at ease. She took her spoon and neatly clipped the top off her boiled egg. She began to say her few words of Greek, her pronunciation careful, while the children giggled and corrected her. When they repeated her English, however, they imitated her accent exactly, like a couple of parrots.

Angela then said, "I am eating my egg," and proceeded to do so.

Crista repeated the phrase in Greek, managing to smear egg on her face.

Miki reprimanded his sister and proudly finished his without mishap.

Angela devised a little game they could play, in Greek and English, and both children began to squeal with glee, while Angela made faces and said things to make them laugh.

A shadow suddenly fell across the table. Angela looked up, flustered, to see Alex standing there.

"I see you rise early, Miss Blair."

"No, not always," Angela replied tremulously. "Perhaps the jet lag, the unfamiliar surroundings . . ."

"Isn't your bed comfortable?"

"Yes, yes, very comfortable," she assured him. As she hesitated and stumbled over her words she felt furious with herself. What a fool he must think her. She simply couldn't relax under his probing, ironic gaze. Her earlier feeling of ease with the children had completely vanished. They, however, refused to remain on the sidelines for long, and they began to regale their father with what English they had learned.

Alex smiled at them—a smile that lit up his features, softening the contours of his face. Suddenly Angela had an impulse to please him so that he would smile at her like that. But it couldn't be, she reminded herself glumly. Petra was the recipient of those dazzling smiles.

As the children grew boisterous, Alex rapped on the table and spoke firmly to them in Greek until they subsided. "They are difficult," he remarked to Angela. "You may find it tedious to give them lessons."

"In that case I'll make the lessons informal," she replied, her equilibrium restored by the impersonal turn of the conversation. "I don't think they're difficult at all, Mr. Pallas. To me they seem quite delightful, and so quick to learn."

"Mmm," he grunted skeptically. "At any rate they've eaten their breakfast, for once."

Angela was disturbed by the autocratic tendency in Alex that extended from women to children—which was the very opposite of her own approach. "The children seem healthy and sturdy," she said. "I'm sure they eat as much as they need. Children are like puppies, really—"

"Like puppies. Exactly. And if you don't watch them every moment, they chew up all the wrong things. I am a firm believer, Miss Blair, in discipline, guidance, and restraint." Alex took a sip of coffee and looked challengingly at Angela.

In spite of her pounding heart, she was caught up in the discussion. "I agree up to a point, but the authoritarian approach needs to be tempered with understanding and love in order to have the desired result. Otherwise, children obey out of fear, and then they lose their wonderful spontaneity—"

"Rubbish. Children are little savages and they need to be tamed. And properly fed. These two have been indifferent eaters, ever since my wife—" He bit his lip suddenly and fell silent.

Angela didn't know what to say. She covered her embarrassment by rushing ahead to expound her theories. "Learning is a game, really. Children have a natural curiosity, and as long as it isn't stifled or they aren't forced—"

"Oh, I see. You believe in anarchy in the classroom," Alex said derisively, his composure restored. "Let the little savages run wild, is that it?"

"No, not at all. You're twisting my words. I'll illustrate with Crista and Miki. If I had sat them down and told them they were going to learn English, they probably would have pouted with impatience, so I made a game of it."

"Well, perhaps it's all right at this level," Alex granted, irritating Angela by his deprecating tone. "But one cannot learn the classics, philosophy, and mathematics without a disciplined approach—"

"Of course not," Angela agreed warmly. "But they are children, after all. If learning is fun for them now, they'll be able to take more stringent discipline when they're older—"

"Good for you, Angela, you tell him." Stephanie had rushed into the room and flopped breathlessly into her seat. "You should listen to Angela, Alex. She knows everything there is to know about children."

Alex gave his sister a withering look, while Angela quickly said, "It's just my opinion—"

"At least you treat Miki and Crista like human beings," said Stephanie, buttering her roll. "Petra, for instance, thinks children should be seen and not heard."

Not even seen, thought Angela privately, noticing that at the mention of Petra's name both children made a face and thrust out their tongues at each other.

Their father reprimanded them sharply.

Angela said nothing more to Alex on the subject of

41

teaching, knowing it was pointless to argue with such a man. However, she felt protective toward Miki and Crista and feared they would be in for a difficult time when he married Petra.

"Today, Alex," Stephanie was saying, "I'm going to take Angela to the Archaeological Museum, and in the afternoon we'll see the Acropolis.

"*Kaliméra*," Savvas mumbled, entering the room and rubbing his eyes like a sleepy child. "I will be your courier, Angela. Today I am entirely at your disposal."

"No, my dear, hard-working brother," Alex contradicted sarcastically, "this morning you are entirely at the disposal of Pallas Enterprises, if you will be so kind. We will combine a tour of the editorial offices with a visit to the Leonidas Printing Plant, so that perhaps you may see a connection that leads to the finished products in the warehouse, which go onto one of our ships in Piraeus, where we will also be stopping. . . ."

"Leonidas, that's Petra's family," Stephanie whispered to Angela. "They do all our printing and own a paper factory as well, which is why Papa always wanted a family connection by marriage."

Angel understood only too well, but her sinking heart lifted when she saw the unhappy pout on Savvas's face. At that moment he looked exactly like Miki, and she could only laugh at him.

Savvas then laughed at himself. "Never mind, Angela. This afternoon we will storm the Acropolis. Don't say no, Alex. You don't want these girls at the mercy of those fellows that cluster there waiting to pounce on unescorted beauties." He lapsed into Greek, causing Stephanie to laugh at his remarks. Even Alex smiled mockingly but did not appropriate Savvas for the afternoon.

42

* * *

As Angela slid into the small English car next to Stephanie, her friend smiled happily. "At last we'll have some time alone, and you can see how well I drive. So tell me, Angelamou," she continued, slyly imitating Savvas as she maneuvered the car through the noisy streets, "what do you think of us all?"

"What a question," said Angela, laughing. "Next to you, my favorites are the children, of course. And Savvas is such a lot of fun. He's a lot like you, Steph."

"And Alex? Does he frighten you?"

"No, not really. He's very—well, sure of himself," Angela said, trying to be diplomatic. "I'm sure he runs the business very well," she finished lamely.

How could she tell her friend what she truly felt? That Alex's very presence in the same room was electrifying. That his low voice thrilled her, and that when he stood close to her, her very skin tingled with pinpricks of fire.

"At least you stood up to Alex, and that's more than most people dare," said Stephanie, breaking in upon Angela's thoughts. "But his reaction to you surprises me. I expected him to—well, never mind. Oh, tonight we're dining at the home of Petros Lampari, a prominent banker and industrialist. I hope you've brought an evening dress with you."

Angela had, and she described it eagerly, glad to change the subject. But after a brief digression Stephanie returned to it. "Savvas adores you, of course, but he must grow up, finally. If only he weren't so devil-may-care. He drives Alex wild. He must master the technical side of the business—computers, something like that. I don't understand anything of it. I only hope Savvas will be conscientious. . . ."

They talked about Pallas Publishing, and by the time they had pulled into the parking lot at the muse-

43

um, Angela was feeling more relaxed and at ease. "It's so wonderful to see you again, Steph," she said impulsively, giving her friend a hug.

Stephanie smiled. "You're flattering me, so it probably means you've fallen in love with my Niko."

This was the subject Angela had dreaded, and she tried to keep her expression bright and positive. "Only a little," she said softly, "but I don't stand a chance."

"Silly, don't tell me that. I know my Niko very well. You mustn't mind if he flirts a little. He's more truly Greek than my brothers, and more old-fashioned. He's traveled in Europe and the Middle East but has so far avoided England and America. I'm afraid he's sort of prejudiced against Anglo-Saxons, especially when it comes to women. And he can be awfully serious at times. We're so different. I suppose that's why I love him so much. Whenever I do something careless or wild, Niko is there to keep me in line." Stephanie laughed merrily, linking arms with Angela as they walked from the car. "I need someone like Niko. If he were like Savvas, for example, we'd just rush off together into a rainbow and never be seen again."

Angela fervently hoped that Stephanie wouldn't be rushing into an abyss with Niko.

"I'm not at all jealous of the way Niko stares at you," Stephanie added, making Angela jump guiltily. "In fact, I'd be angry if he didn't think you were beautiful."

Angela remained silent. Niko certainly thought something about her, but Angela doubted that he was concerned with her appearance. Could it simply be her "Anglo-Saxon" quality that made him treat her as if she were his enemy? Angela couldn't bring up the matter with Stephanie—at least not now. Her friend was so happy that she couldn't bear to destroy her joyful mood. Angela's suspicions were probably unfounded anyway.

At the Archaeological Museum Angela lost herself in wonder and excitement. The museum was enormous, so they concentrated on a few of the exhibits. Stephanie pulled Angela by the hand into what she called the "golden room." Here were the sensational excavations of the famous archaeologist Schliemann in the 1870s from the royal tombs of Mycenae. Angela was awestruck by the incredible artistry of those craftsmen who had lived in the Bronze Age. They had created such exquisite artifacts of gold—bowls, cups, and even masks for the dead.

They moved on to admire the sculptures. "Here, Ange, are the most famous classical statues. Here is Zeus, poised to throw a thunderbolt."

Angela's attention, however, was caught by a statue a few feet beyond where Stephanie was pointing. Stepping closer to the marble sculpture, Angela felt her heart give a small flutter. It could only be Apollo. Although the face was not as handsome or well preserved as the photo that looked so much like Alex Pallas, this statue had the same proud bearing, the same divine aspect. . . .

"Goodness, you're staring at that as if you'd like to bring it to life," Stephanie observed.

Angela flushed, tearing her eyes away guiltily.

Stephanie looked at her strangely but did not press the point.

"This is the best time to view the Acropolis," Savvas told Angela that afternoon as he bought their tickets. "It's cooler but still light enough to see the actual workmanship, how they put stone upon stone, pillar upon pillar. Look at the marks left by the wheels of the chariots. They were brilliant, my ancestors, don't you think?"

Savvas gave Angela a hug, and she responded with a smile. She did hope that he and Stephanie wouldn't chatter too much. This was an experience Angela wanted to have for herself in peace, even though, in contradiction of her purpose, she had pleaded that Miki and Crista be allowed to come with them.

"They'll be too tired," Stephanie had protested.

"Oh, let's drag them along," Savvas had said, siding with Angela. "Let them see it before all the air pollution wrecks in fifty years what has been standing for more than two thousand."

Angela felt like a tiny, insignificant speck in the universe as she came up the worn marble steps and went through the huge columns of the magnificent Propylaea. The Parthenon was as majestic as any picture of it Angela had ever seen, and she was awed as she strolled among the columns of honey-colored marble.

"Here," said Savvas softly, taking her arm, "is where Athena was worshiped. Of course this place used to be filled with sculptures and whatnots. By the way, all the ancient Greek statues were painted in bright colors. Only time has taken away the paint and left everything so pure and white, which is much better, don't you agree?"

When Savvas and Angela came up to the Caryatids, the six regal stone maidens in carved robes holding up more than two tons of marble on their heads, they found Crista and Miki staring at them with open mouths. The children fired questions at Stephanie.

"Crista wants to know where their arms are, and Miki thinks they must have a terrible headache," said Stephanie, giggling.

Crista began to jump up and down, asking for a

46

lemonade. "I'll be at the café down there with the children," Stephanie said. "I'm sure you want to walk around some more."

Savvas took Angela's arm. "Come with me." He led her around the side of the Erechtheum, smaller than the Parthenon and extremely graceful with its thin Ionic columns.

"We will rest for a moment here in the shade of the porch and admire the view," he said, staring appreciatively at Angela.

"The view is that way," Angela remarked, inclining her head.

"For you, yes. For me there is nothing more beautiful to look at here or anywhere than you."

Embarrassed by his effusiveness, even though she didn't take it seriously, Angela turned and looked out at the mountains. "What is that called, the tallest one?"

"Mount Parnis," Savvas murmured, kissing Angela's cheek and then the tip of her earlobe, sending a slight shiver through her.

She tried to move away, but he had an arm about her firmly. "You smell of flowers and sun. And your yellow hair is like spun gold. If you had lived in those ancient times, they would have built a temple to worship the beautiful Angela."

"Please, Savvas," implored Angela, smiling and squirming at the same time. "I'm trying to experience the grandeur of the monuments."

Her words made him laugh, and he released her with a kiss on the forehead. "I don't blame you. And here is this clown separating you from the wonders of history with a few paltry kisses. But very truly meant, Angelamou." He even managed to look serious for a moment before laughing once again.

47

"Let's join Steph and the children," Angela said. "I'm rather thirsty myself."

"As for me," Savvas sighed, "I can drink in your eyes, which are the color the sky is turning just now, starting from Mount Hymettus and spreading over the Attic plain." He tried to kiss her lips, but she managed to twist out of his arms.

Savvas laughed. "I'll let you go now, Angelamou, but sometime soon . . ." He followed her down the ancient steps toward the café.

Chapter Four

Stephanie rapped on Angela's door. "Are you packed? I probably forgot to tell you that we're leaving for our island after the dinner party tonight. Just throw your stuff in your bags. Yianni will carry them to the car."

"Who is Yianni?" Angela asked, fearful that yet another Pallas brother had turned up.

"Maria's husband, of course. Oh, do hurry, Ange." Stephanie clattered down the stairs.

Angela had no chance to plead for more time. As usual, Stephanie had omitted to tell her that they were leaving the house so early. Angela had only just showered, and her hair was wet. It was so thick and heavy that it needed at least half an hour of steady brushing to dry smooth and silky down to her shoulders. But she could not keep everyone waiting. Rubbing her hair vigorously with her towel, she squeezed out as much dampness as possible. Then she dressed.

Almost a year before, Angela had bought an evening dress in Boston on impulse. She seldom had the occasion to dress formally in Springport, but she had so loved the dress that she had not been able to resist it. It was only now as she put it on that she realized it had a Greek motif, and probably that was what had attracted her in the first place. Of cream-colored silk jersey, it was sleeveless and completely pleated, falling in shimmering, clinging folds against her slender form.

There was a cord of matching material that tied around the waist.

When she looked in the mirror, she flushed because she appeared to have dressed deliberately to look like an ancient goddess. Her hair, curling damply down to her shoulders, with soft tendrils over her forehead, completed the look.

"Angela, come on!" Stephanie called from the bottom of the stairs.

Hastily Angela flung clothes from drawers and closet into her suitcases. Glancing quickly at her face, Angela used a light lip blusher and dabbed a little eye shadow on her lids, darkening her long, thick lashes with brown mascara. She needed nothing else, for her face and arms were already tanned.

Angela jumped as a knock sounded at her door. Opening it, she saw a small, middle-aged man standing there, crinkling his face in a smile as he bid the *despinis* good evening.

He carried out her bags, and Angela, feeling desperately self-conscious, followed him down the majestic staircase.

When she came to the door of the drawing room, everyone was already assembled. Stephanie, wearing a crimson silk dress which set off her shiny black hair, reclined in a big chair. Niko, in a pale blue dinner jacket, was casually draped over the arm.

Petra was wearing a black dress that was completely backless, and almost frontless. Her hair was piled on her head Grecian style, and she wore a fabulous necklace with a diamond as big as a peach pit glittering in her cleavage.

Angela owned little jewelry. Having nothing, really, to go with her dress, she was without any ornament. She couldn't see Alex, but Savvas was standing with his back to the door, looking uncharacteristically formal in a rose-colored dinner jacket.

When Angela, taking a deep breath, walked into the room, all conversation ceased abruptly. Everyone turned to look at her, and she grew immediately warm and stiff under their scrutiny. The dress was all right, surely, but if she had only had time to do something with her hair. . . .

Niko ran his eyes insolently from the top of her head, lingering at her dress, and sliding down to her feet, encased in delicate gold-strapped sandals.

Savvas, turning, looked stunned, and then muttered in Greek, his face breaking into an incredulous smile, "Angelamou, my golden beauty." He kissed her solemnly on both cheeks. "You are breathtaking," he whispered, stepping back to regard her.

Petra, aiming her iceberg eyes at Angela, looked as if she could cheerfully stab her to the heart. Angela did not dare to glance at Alex directly, but her fingers began to tremble when she felt his eyes on her.

Perceiving her friend's shyness, Stephanie came forward to take her hand. "Angela, you have absolutely outdone yourself. The dress, your hair, everything," she murmured. "Have a glass of champagne. We were toasting the success of Pallas Enterprises. Ever since Alex took over we have expanded and diversified and everything is going wonderfully well."

Maria handed Angela a glass, smiling and murmuring, "Polí oréa."

"That means 'very beautiful,'" explained Alex in a low voice, staring broodingly at Angela. "Stin iyá sas —to your health," he said, raising his glass in a toast.

Angela, gripping the stem tightly in her nervousness, had a sip of the bubbling liquid. Daring to look at last at Alex, she felt her face flush mercilessly. His eyes were boring into her very soul, the expression intense and rather sullen.

Stephanie insisted upon lending Angela a necklace to go with the dress, and she rushed upstairs to get it, although Niko called after her that there wasn't time.

Standing nervously off to one side, Angela kept her glass to her lips, her eyes lowered. Through her thick lashes she observed that Petra had stepped in front of Alex, claiming his attention, and was talking to him loudly in English of their mutual friends who would be at the party.

Savvas moved to Angela's side. "You are nothing less than a goddess, Angelamou," he murmured, "and so beautifully tanned after only one day. Not half-cooked, like most foreigners."

Angela laughed nervously and drained her glass, whereupon Savvas immediately rushed for more champagne.

Finally Stephanie returned with her necklace, a reproduction of an ancient motif of irregular, almost square shapes in hammered gold hanging like charms on a gold chain.

"Here, I'll fasten it," declared Savvas eagerly, grabbing the necklace from his sister. In his haste he dropped his champagne.

Angela jumped back, just missing having it spill on her dress, while Savvas cursed his clumsiness. Fortunately the thick Persian carpet kept the delicate crystal from shattering. As Savvas tried to fasten the necklace, he dropped it as well.

"Allow me," said Alex in an ironic tone, kneeling to retrieve the necklace from the floor.

He stood up, his nearness to Angela causing her breath to come in short gasps and her heart to thump relentlessly behind her ribs.

Stepping behind her, Alex fastened the necklace himself. As soon as Angela felt his burning fingers on the nape of her neck, an involuntary shudder passed through her.

"Oh, that's gorgeous!" exclaimed Stephanie, clapping her hands. "Oh, just look, Ange," she implored, pulling her by the hand to the gilt-framed mirror.

It was certainly a magnificent necklace, but Angela deplored her flushed face and her curling hair, and wished she were anywhere else in the world at this moment. She had never felt so self-conscious.

Alex, tearing his gaze from Angela, had engaged the other two men in conversation, and Angela could glance at him from the corner of her eye without being conspicuous. He wore a cream-colored dinner jacket, a frilly shirt with pearl studs, and a black tie. She was disturbed to note that he looked as prepossessing in formal clothes as in informal ones, and was the only man of the three who appeared at ease. Savvas, his face scrubbed shiny, looked like a boy dressed for a part, while Niko's glowering, foreign looks made him seem out of place in such western attire.

Petra approached Angela, her icy eyes chilling her with their malevolence.

"I hear you're becoming a second mother to the children," she announced in her throaty voice, which Angela was sure she had deliberately cultivated for dramatic effect. "Tell me, when are you going to marry that lawyer of yours and have children of your own?"

"Oh, Petra, really!" Stephanie admonished sharply. She cast Angela a look of compassion, while Petra, ignoring Stephanie, walked regally away.

"Don't mind her, Angela. She's just jealous of you. She'd like to be blond herself and in fact, once bleached her hair. It looked so awful with her muddy complexion that she had to dye it black again."

Angela was aware that Stephanie did not care for Petra, but she didn't dare discuss the other woman with her friend. If Petra was Stephanie's future sister-in-law it would be better to keep her feelings to herself.

When they arrived at the Lampari mansion, in the seaside suburb of Lagonissi, Angela was struck by the view from the car window. The house was on a hill and looked out at the sea. As Niko helped Angela alight from the car he squeezed her hand familiarly.

Angela shrank from the contact, all her apprehension of him returning with a rush. She was determined to stay as far away from him as possible.

The house was elegant and richly furnished, mostly with French antiques. Costa Lampari and his wife were a middle-aged couple, very sophisticated and welcoming. Angela was so bewildered by the large numbers of people that she forgot each name as she heard it. Like most educated Greeks, the guests spoke fluent English and French, and Angela felt at a disadvantage. She was grateful for Savvas's presence because the looks various men were giving her made her flush with shyness. "You see, Angelamou, I am not the only one who finds you irresistible. If I were not here to protect you, they would eat you alive."

Savvas exaggerated. Still, never in her life had Angela been devoured by such glances as these rich, worldly Greeks cast upon her.

After more champagne Angela found herself able to relax somewhat. Most of the women, years older than Angela, were friendly and curious about her background, and many of them had been to America.

The guests were not all Greek, Angela discovered. She was introduced to a French painter and afterward an Italian filmmaker of some renown. At his side was a flamboyantly attractive champagne-blond, the star of his famous films, who was also his wife. This fact did not stop the director from staring with frank interest at Angela and asking her if she had ever acted.

"No," she said diffidently, remembering the unrewarded efforts of her college drama teacher.

The director's wife, tugging at his arm in petulant jealousy, ended the little exchange. Later, however, the Italian accosted Angela and whispered, "If ever you change your mind, here is my card." He pressed it into her hand and slipped away to rejoin his wife. Angela felt truly flattered, since she had thought very highly of the few films of his she had seen in Boston.

Publishing was only one of the Pallas interests, Angela learned in the course of the evening. As Stephanie had begun to explain earlier, since Alex had taken over the family business two years earlier, it had been expanded to encompass shipping, banking, and mining exploration. Angela began to realize that the Pallas family was even wealthier than she had earlier imagined.

At dinner the seating was arranged by their hosts, so Angela had no choice but to sit between Niko and Alex. Petra was on Alex's other side, claiming all his attention, while Stephanie was placed next to Niko, too far away for Angela to talk to her. Savvas sat across the table, flanked by two lovely young ladies, but he preferred to flirt with Angela.

"How do you like Greek food?" Niko suddenly asked Angela. Every time he spoke to her it was like an attack.

"I do, very much. I used to have Greek meals oc-

casionally in Boston, although it was not as authen-
tic—"

"With your boyfriend?"

"Uh, yes," Angela whispered, uncomfortable.

The expression in Niko's eyes was insolent and an-
tagonistic. "He is a lawyer, is he not? Rich?"

"No, no, not at all," she said hastily, coloring. "I
mean he's a lawyer, yes, but not rich. He's comfortable,
reasonably successful, but Springport is a very small
town—"

"You mean you will not be rich when you marry?"
Niko's eyes grazed her face with hostility.

Angela was having difficulty eating her lobster, and
Niko's insinuations didn't help. The conversation was
distressing, with everyone taking her marriage for
granted.

"You need some help, I believe," said Alex, noticing
her clumsiness with her fork. He leaned over her plate
and deftly removed the meat from her lobster claw.
When his arm brushed hers, she had to grip the edge
of her chair to keep from trembling noticeably.

Mutely she watched Alex's hands in fascination.
They were slender, with long fingers, strong and de-
cisive. She wondered what it would be like if he were
to stroke her hair, and she felt herself blushing fiercely.
Her confusion increased when she saw that Niko was
glaring at her.

"All right now?" Alex asked in his low, exciting
voice.

"Yes, thank you," she replied in a husky whisper.
Her heart was pounding relentlessly.

By the time a big bowl of fruit was set before them
Angela felt she could not eat another morsel. Savvas,
however, insisted on reaching across the table with
small pieces of watermelon on the tip of his knife.

56

"Come, Angela, you must eat up."

"Savvas always did like fat women," Petra remarked spitefully, staring at Angela with cold envy.

Whenever Petra said something outrageous to Angela, Alex pretended not to have heard. At least, the expression on his face never altered. But outspoken Stephanie wouldn't let Petra get away with such a vicious remark. "Angela, fat? Never. She can eat anything and never gain half a kilo, the lucky thing. All through college I was on a constant diet, and she ate her portions and mine. Still, she was voted most beautiful girl four years in a row."

"Of course she was," concurred Savvas, as if there could be no doubt. "Just one piece more, Angelamou."

"Watch out your knife doesn't cut her tongue," snapped Petra in a tone that suggested she hoped the opposite.

"Watch out for your own tongue," retorted Savvas.

Niko said something angrily in Greek over Angela's back, and she saw from the corner of her eye that Alex smiled mockingly at him.

After dinner there was dancing to the music of a small orchestra in the exquisite drawing room and the guests spilled out through the French doors onto the terrace. It was a clear night, the sky brilliant with stars, and a heady breeze blew off the water.

Angela felt like Cinderella at the ball, especially when Savvas danced with her, twirling her around and whispering words of flattery into her ear.

Alex was dancing with Petra. Try as she might, Angela could not help being constantly aware of Alex every minute of the evening—of where he was standing, what he was doing, whom he was talking to, or looking at.

57

In the course of the dancing their eyes caught and locked for one breathless minute. Angela felt weak in the knees and became terribly frightened of her feelings. She longed to be in Alex's arms, to dance with him out of the room, onto the terrace, and far up into the starry sky.

Idiot, she reviled herself silently. As if Alex Pallas cared two pins about her! To him she was simply another American girl of the type he sneered at, independent and unwilling to be ordered around like a piece of chattel by the lord of the manor. It would be a hellish experience to be his wife, Angela told herself fiercely. Then she wondered what had, in fact, happened to Miki and Crista's mother. She wanted to ask Stephanie, and yet she hesitated.

Although Greeks might be very outspoken and unabashed in their curiosity, Angela had been raised to feel a certain reticence about prying into personal affairs. Her Aunt Emily had discouraged such questions. "It's not polite to ask, dear," she had told her niece. "If someone wants to tell you, they will."

When two men in turn asked Savvas if they might dance with Angela, he reluctantly agreed. She felt most peculiar that Savvas's permission was required and not her own. Apparently what she thought was of no concern.

Her fears were allayed when her partners held her some distance away, quite correctly, and made polite conversation. She flushed to think that she was considered Savvas's property, and marveled at the archaic rules that still governed the relationships between men and women in this country.

Alex danced only with Petra, but Angela felt his eye upon her several times when she was in the arms of her partners. She began to feel warm and flushed from the dancing, and as soon as the number had drawn to a close, she excused herself and walked to the end of the patio. Stepping to one side so that she would not be noticed from the house, Angela looked out at the sea.

A damp breeze was blowing in her direction, and she could smell the mingled odor of salt and seaweed. In fascination, Angela watched the graceful flight patterns of the white gulls as they silently swooped and soared over the foamy waves breaking like lace on the beach.

"Here you are, my beauty," Savvas said, hurrying to her side and putting his arm around her shoulders. "It is a beautiful sight, isn't it?"

"Oh, yes. But I'm surprised that the gulls are so quiet. Back home they screech constantly."

"Ah, but here the people do the screeching, so it is only fitting that the sea gulls are silent," said Alex's voice in back of them.

He was standing so close behind Angela that she could feel his breath ruffling her hair. A tremor went down her back, and she covered her feelings by laughing at his remark.

Savvas stirred impatiently at her side, but he removed his arm from her shoulder. In spite of his bravado, Savvas seemed to be quite in awe of his older brother—not that Angela could blame him. Alex Pallas had a commanding presence that might make a stronger man than Savvas quail. As head of the family, Alex undoubtedly asserted his power. Savvas, still a student, probably had no means of his own and was dependent upon his brother.

"It is time for us to depart," Alex now said. "Come, Miss Blair." He took her elbow and propelled her firmly, while a sulky Savvas walked on her other side.

When they took their leave, Angela was surprised at the way Costa Lampari and his wife embraced her, kissing her warmly and expressing their wish that they would see much more of her.

Petra came flying up to them, proclaiming in loud tones that they must be guests at her house very soon. In spite of Petra's invitation and intimate way of speaking to them, Angela sensed that the Lamparis were not particularly fond of her.

Savvas helped Angela into the limousine, making sure that she sat near the window and that he was next to her, his arm around her, claiming all her attention.

Angela sighed several times. Her vacation was turning out to be very different from what she had expected. Stephanie had been her main reason for coming to Greece. Yet, not only did she see very little of her friend, but she was made to feel defensive by all three men who were constantly present.

A further complication was Angela's inability to be totally open and honest with Stephanie. She could barely bring herself to talk about Rory. Stephanie, naturally enough, assumed that Angela adored him as much as she herself loved Niko. And Niko was an additional barrier in the friendship. Increasingly, Angela thought it would be better to return home at once.

But how could she get out of going to the island with them? She would be too humiliated to ask the chauffeur to stop the car, take her back to Athens, and put her in a hotel. Her aunt had always told her not to "make a fuss." And yet, wouldn't there be an even greater fuss if she allowed herself to be brought to the island and there be captive to Savvas's attentions, Niko's hostility, and Alex's disdainful mockery? Besides, Petra would be there as well. Like most Greek girls of good families, Petra did not work. She would be with the Pallas family all summer.

Actually, it was too late for Angela to do anything at all, since they had arrived at the harbor of Piraeus. Before she could catch her breath Angela found herself on the quay, ringed with beautiful yachts, while the chauffeur was sent on his way back to Athens.

"Angela, Angela!" Startled, she turned and saw Crista waving and shouting to her from the deck of the biggest yacht of all, a lovely two-masted schooner. The name *Crysula* was painted in big letters on the side.

"Isn't she fabulous?" Stephanie squeezed Angela's arm. "She's named after Mother."

Angela nodded, watching with mixed feelings as her bags were carried aboard by Yianni.

"She sleeps twelve, Angela," Savvas was saying. "Now, let's see how we will arrange it—"

"Don't overtax your brain, Brother," interrupted Alex. "I have already decided. In one cabin, Crista, Stephanie, Petra, and Angela. In the small double, Yianni and Maria. Niko will share with me, and you, Savvas, can share a cabin with Miki."

"That will make for stimulating conversation," Savvas said petulantly.

"In that case you can spend your time sailing instead of shirking your duties as usual."

Angela didn't care for the ironic tone Alex took with his brother. Just because Alex seemed unable to enjoy himself was no reason for him to deplore Savvas's happy disposition. In addition, she was dismayed to be stuck in the same cabin with Petra, and didn't understand why the children had been separated. At the same time, she was still recovering from the thrill at hearing Alex refer to her as "Angela" for the first time.

The boat's white sails contrasted dramatically with the polished dark wood of the hull and deck. Angela had never been aboard such a magnificent vessel. Down below, the cabins were cozy and contained comfortable bunks. Crista jumped up and down on hers in excitement, chattering in Greek to Angela and Stephanie.

But when Petra, a forced smile on her lips, spoke to Crista, the child shook her head and hid her face in her pillow. Petra's look of cold fury at having been spurned drew an instant reaction from Stephanie. "Never mind, Petra, it's the father you have to charm. Children are not so easily deceived."

Petra grew even angrier and spoke sharply in Greek to Stephanie, her eyes blazing. Stephanie retorted in kind. From the way both glanced at her, Angela had the feeling that she was somehow involved in the argument.

Much later, when Angela could tell from their regular breathing that her cabin mates were asleep, she lay wide awake in her bunk with her unquiet thoughts. She was thinking about Petra, now understanding why Alex might have balked originally at marrying such a spiteful creature, beautiful or not. Even more strange was that he could contemplate marrying her now, when it was so obvious that she disliked his children and that the feeling was mutual. What had happened to his wife?

There were no answers to be found in Angela's aching head, and she decided to go up on deck. Slipping softly out of bed, she put on her long pale blue robe and crept up the stairs.

The sight from the deck stirred her. Overhead thousands of stars glittered, casting a muted reflection on the inky water, which lapped gently at the sides of the boat, gliding smoothly through the surf. The steady breeze whipped Angela's hair back from her face.

"Angela, what is it?" Savvas had come upon her so quietly that she jumped. "Don't be afraid. I didn't mean to frighten you. Can't sleep, eh? Why not?"

"I—I don't know. The excitement, perhaps. Savvas, where exactly is your island?"

"In the Cyclades. It means circle, and is so called because the islands circle the sacred island of Delos, birthplace of Apollo and Artemis. And then there is Mykonos, Paros, and Santorin. Our island is small and covered with jasmine, a wonderful, sweet-smelling flower but not sweeter than you." He put his arm around her shoulders, and nuzzled her hair with his nose.

"Aren't you supposed to be sailing this boat?"

"Of course I am sailing her, but I have set the automatic pilot for a moment. Don't worry, it is a very calm night. She can't go off course."

"But you are, a bit," Angela teased him as she moved out of his embrace.

"I see that you don't like me at all," Savvas said sulkily, looking at her like a baleful puppy.

"Of course I like you. I just wish that you would talk more and hug less. You make me feel like a rag doll."

Savvas threw back his head and laughed. "You are a doll, anyway, *kúkla mu*, but I will try to do as you wish. If only your eyes did not look as if they were scooped out of the sea, your lips like the luscious little strawberries that grow wild on the island—eh!" Savvas shrugged and then wound his arms insistently around her. "I can't help it, Angela, I adore you."

She felt his warm lips against her ear, while his curling eyelash fluttered against her cheek.

When she averted her face so that he could not find her lips, he contented himself with covering her cheek and forehead with his soft kisses.

63

In spite of herself, Angela rather liked such affection and felt that there wasn't any harm in it.

Suddenly a cold voice said something in Greek behind them.

Savvas released Angela and spun around to face a very angry Alex.

"So this is how you sail the boat! My small son would show more responsibility."

"Pah, this boat sails herself. Anyway, I have only been here two seconds," muttered Savvas, slinking back to his post.

For a moment Alex glared at Angela with hard, luminous eyes, forcing her to drop her own gaze in embarrassment. "I—I'm sorry if I—if I distracted him. I couldn't sleep so I came up for some air and—and Savvas—"

"Yes," said Alex icily, "I saw."

Angela was momentarily piqued. What was he so angry about? Her harmless flirtation with Savvas had nothing to do with him.

"Why can't you sleep?" Alex asked her gruffly after a moment.

"I don't know." She pushed her tangled curls off her face and rubbed her forehead.

"Headache?" he asked in a softer voice. "You're not, perhaps, accustomed to champagne?"

Angela nodded in answer to both questions. "I'll go down now—"

"Wait. Come here." His voice was low once again and sent a shiver through her, but she remained where she was.

Alex compressed his lips at her refusal to obey him and drew closer to her himself. He was wearing a light Windbreaker but no shirt. The jacket was open, and she could see his bare bronzed chest.

"Turn around," he commanded.

While a part of her rebelled at doing his bidding, she found herself following his order as if in a trance.

When she turned and put her hands on the railing, Alex came behind her and began very gently to massage her forehead. "Shut your eyes," he said, his voice low, hypnotic. "Relax. Think of something pleasant and restful. A meadow full of flowers under a bright sun. Or this boat gliding through the water and keeping a rhythm with the waves."

Angela could feel his low, compelling voice vibrate in his chest as he gently moved her back until she was leaning against him. When he bent his head and kissed the curls on top of her head, Angela trembled and her knees grew wobbly. She started to sway, and felt his arm slide around her waist to steady her. He held her thus for one delirious moment. "Don't be afraid, I won't let you fall," he murmured. Then he turned her around and, putting one hand on her shoulder, tilted her chin up with the other. She looked straight into his eyes and saw that they were regarding her with an intensity she had never before experienced. Slowly his face drew closer to her own.

Suddenly the boat gave a lurch, and Savvas could be heard yelling in Greek.

Abruptly Alex released Angela, calling something to his brother and shaking his head in exasperation. "I must show that fool what to do when the wind shifts. You are all right?"

"Yes," she murmured doubtfully.

"Good. Then you must sleep now. *Kalinikhta,* Angela." He turned quickly and left her.

Chapter Five

When Angela went up on deck early, before any of her cabin mates were awake, she saw Niko, Alex, and Savvas lowering the white sails and putting up a spinnaker—a scooplike sail of thin material in bright stripes of orange, yellow, and purple.

Having often sailed with Rory at the Cape, Angela knew that the spinnaker was designed to make the boat go faster. She thought it looked beautiful, gaily flapping in the wind. Suddenly she felt lighthearted and happy, enjoying the jaunty motion of the boat, the pale blue sky, and the friendly, hot Sun beaming down upon her.

Angela was wearing her bikini under her sundress, but she hesitated to remove the dress in front of the three men. She decided to sunbathe on the port side, as far from their view as she could get.

Just as she finished rubbing her arms and legs with suntan lotion, Stephanie joined her, a merry smile brightening her features. "You're an early bird this morning. Here, let me do your back."

A few moments later, watching Angela lying on her stomach, her long, shapely legs fully extended, Stephanie sighed. "Ange, you haven't changed a bit. How you keep your figure so slender, but at the same time so sexy—"

"Please, Steph," Angela demurred. "My figure is nothing special."

"It certainly is, and if you were less modest, you'd know it. Ah, to have had some Anglo-Saxon ancestors." Stephanie sighed again. "Height and longer legs are what I need. Instead, I'm built so close to the ground I resemble a dachshund."

"Oh, Steph, you don't." Angela laughed. "I think you're lovely, and—and so does Niko." She hoped Stephanie hadn't heard the slight hesitation in her voice. Still, Niko surely did care for Stephanie. Why else would he be marrying her? Money, said an evil voice within her, but she dismissed it impatiently. As one of the top directors of Pallas Enterprises, Niko surely had more than enough.

Angela turned to lie on her back, determined to stop her idle speculations and enjoy the warmth of the morning Sun on her skin.

Suddenly she felt eyes upon her. Angela fluttered her eyes open slightly. Alex, perched halfway up a rope ladder, was adjusting the spinnaker, but his body was twisted and she was sure he was staring at her behind his dark glasses. Near the railing was Niko, coiling rope, and he, too, was glancing in her direction.

Savvas came rushing up, stopping short in front of Angela and blocking the Sun. He exclaimed in Greek and knelt on the mat, whispering, "Oh, my beauty, the more of you I see, the more of you I love. But come and look now. There is our island."

From the railing Angela could see a low, barren mountain in the distance, a sandy beach in front, and clusters of green—trees, she supposed—between the craggy mountain and the beach.

They dropped anchor close to shore and Alex rowed the women and children the rest of the way in the small dinghy, while Niko and Savvas swam the distance.

Sitting facing Alex, Angela grew flustered. She thought of the way he had massaged her forehead on deck, of how he had turned her to face him. He had kissed the top of her head tenderly. Had he been about to kiss her lips?

Stop thinking such foolishness, she told herself fiercely, knowing that she was blushing. She hoped that Alex was not noticing her at all but concentrating on his rowing. She could not see his eyes behind the dark glasses but his presence, in only a swimsuit, quite rattled her. His smooth, darkly tanned skin gleamed like that of the bronze Apollo of her picture book. Alex's powerful arms on the oars sent the dinghy gliding effortlessly through the water. Her eyes kept returning to his strong, well-shaped legs firmly braced against both sides of the boat. Fortunately, Crista was squirming all over Angela's knees like a little puppy, and she was able to pretend she wasn't looking at Alex at all.

Savvas was waiting on the beach to greet them. "How do you like the island, Angela? Isn't it beautiful?" Without waiting for her reply he pointed proudly. "It has everything an island should have, in miniature: mountains, beaches, olive trees, pine trees, lemon and orange trees. Here, Angela, I have made you a bouquet of jasmine."

He handed her a sprig of delicate stems with glossy oval green leaves and white flowers, each consisting of five flat petals that felt velvety to the touch. Angela was immediately captivated by the odor, fresh, and at the same time redolent of the exotic East. She imagined that the maidens of *The Arabian Nights* had perfumed themselves with just such an essence.

"Come, Angela, we will climb up there and you will

have a view of the entire island. Notice there are no cars here. Only donkeys are used for transportation."

"Savvas." Alex strode to his brother's side and gripped his shoulder firmly. "This morning we have some business to discuss with Papa. I like to keep him informed of what we are doing, to keep up his interest. You are not here only to have a holiday, remember. Niko can show our visitor the sights. And you, Stephanie, take the children to their grandmother. And see that Maria and Yianni get settled in. We will eat at one," he finished, in a tone that allowed for no contradiction.

Angela quailed at the thought of having to spend any time alone with Niko, but she didn't see how she could escape. Niko immediately began to talk in a conversational tone to her. "The island is only thirteen kilometers by six. We live at the big house, of course, which you'll see later. Then there are about two dozen cottages with the people who work for Pallas, growing vegetables and keeping some goats and chickens. They fish as well, and see to the gardens. That small church on the hill is for them."

Taking her arm insistently, Niko led Angela away from the beach and into a cluster of young pine trees, warmly fragrant from the sun. "We'll rest awhile," he declared, flinging himself down on a carpet of soft pine needles. "Sit."

Angela lowered herself gingerly, as far away from him as she dared without seeming rude.

"A private island. Nice to own one, isn't it?" Niko asked.

"Yes," she murmured doubtfully. She'd seen enough of this fellow to know that he didn't engage in idle chatter. There was surely a point to his question.

"You like Greece, eh? You wouldn't mind living here?"

Angela traced a pattern in the sand with a little twig. "Yes, I like it, but it's a long way from home."

Niko edged closer to her. "That may be, but when one is rich, one can fly here, there, and everywhere as if by magic carpet. Friday in Athens, Saturday in Springport, eh?"

Imperceptibly Angela slid an inch or two away to keep the same distance between them as before. "I don't know what you mean. I certainly don't have the means to pay for traveling back and forth—"

"Exactly. But Savvas is a wealthy young man, is he not? Much richer than the poor boyfriend of the small-town law practice."

Angela felt her face flushing at his nasty insinuations. Jumping nimbly to her feet, she said, "I'd like to go to the house now and freshen up before lunch—"

Before she could think, he had swiftly risen to his feet, moved to her side, and grabbed her arm viciously. "You are evasive to my questions, why? Your boyfriend is not important to you or you would be with him and not playing dangerous games with the Pallas family."

"Let go of me," Angela cried, trying to shake off his steely grip. "I don't know what you're talking about. I'm not playing any kinds of games."

Niko snorted harshly, shaking his curly head at her. "Savvas is a charming boy, a flirtatious boy, but underneath his smiles he is very practical. He would never marry a foreigner with nothing to bring to the family in the way of dowry, see? A few laughs, certainly, a pleasant affair, some idle promises, but afterward—"

"I really don't want to have this conversation," Angela cried, growing angry. "You couldn't be more wrong! You take for granted things that you have no right—"

His hand tightened on her arm, bruising it. "I have every right, as a member of the family, almost." Twisting her arm behind her back suddenly, he reached toward her and tried to kiss her.

Terrified, Angela leaned back so abruptly that she fell to the ground and pulled Niko with her. As soon as she was able to squirm away, and hardly knowing what she was doing, she jumped up and ran blindly, with no idea of direction or destination. She knew only that she had to escape.

After several minutes she was forced to stop and catch her breath. There was a pain in her side, and her forehead was damp with perspiration. She leaned against a tree and tried to calm herself. There was no sign that Niko had attempted to follow her.

Glancing upward, she saw that she was leaning against an olive tree. She recognized the gnarled branches and the silvery green leaves. There were even some tiny budding olives no bigger than the nail on her little finger. She was in an olive grove, so different from anything she had ever before encountered, that she might as well have been on the moon. Still, when she looked at her watch and saw that it was only fifteen minutes to lunchtime, she grew anxious. She did not want to antagonize Alex, but at the moment had no idea as to how far she might be from the house.

Just then she heard the sound of someone coming through the bushes behind the trees. Her heart began to pound. If Niko was going to grab her again . . .

It was Alex. He stood at the edge of the olive grove, staring coolly at her, the breeze ruffling his hair and billowing the sleeves of the blue shirt he was wearing. His face was dark with anger.

"What are you doing here? Is Savvas with you? You haven't even been to the house, although Niko returned ages ago. Never mind; don't bother to excuse

71

yourself. Just come with me. From now on, do your contemplations at a more appropriate hour. My parents do not like to be kept waiting at mealtime."

He whirled and strode through the trees. Angela had to walk very quickly—run, almost—to keep up with him. She felt hot, uncomfortable, and irritated with Alex. He was as bad as Niko in his way. Did all Greeks take one's guilt for granted, never giving a person a chance to explain? What would Alex have thought if he had known the reason for her flight, if he were aware of the attitude Niko took toward her?

She caught her breath as she glimpsed the house, which was not far from the olive grove. It was built on several levels, like a pueblo, in the Cycladic style, with slightly rounded corners and lovely oval arches. The house was so thickly whitewashed that it appeared to Angela like a fairy-tale place covered with white icing.

Alex bounded up the curving front steps, past a front patio, and paused at the door. He turned and gave the breathless Angela a long, brooding look. "I want to speak to you in my study about fifteen minutes after lunch."

Opening the door, he stepped aside and gestured for her to enter, making her a mocking bow.

Feeling smaller than a worm, Angela crept past him.

Stephanie was waiting in the hall to show Angela her room. "Quickly, Ange. You have to put on a dress for lunch. What happened to you?" Stephanie regarded her curiously.

Angela hastily washed and put on a cool pale green sleeveless dress.

"Niko said that one minute you were with him and the next minute you had vanished."

"I—I don't know. We somehow went in different

directions, and I guess I got lost." How Angela's face burned at the falsehood. She was used to speaking the truth, and it distressed her to have to lie like this, especially to her dear Stephanie, from whom she had never in the past had any secrets.

The girls joined the others in a lovely outdoor arbor behind Angela's room. It was a large trellised patio covered by grapevines, from which ripening clusters of green grapes hung invitingly. There was a large oval marble table and outdoor chairs. The rest of the family was already assembled.

Angela was presented to Mr. and Mrs. Pallas, both of whom warmly welcomed her with a kiss on either cheek. Mr. Pallas had a round, smiling face like his daughter and younger son. He seemed quite frail, however, and he didn't speak much, although his bright eyes followed the conversation with interest. Angela guessed that he had once been a vigorous and effective businessman, now, sadly, grown very old.

His much younger wife looked at Angela with probing, observant eyes like Alex's. Her smile also reminded Angela of Alex. Mrs. Pallas wore her still-jet-black hair in a bun at the nape of her neck and gave an overall impression of regal poise.

Neither of the elder Pallases could speak more than two words of English, and Angela regretted that she would be unable to converse with the couple unless she was able to improve her rudimentary knowledge of Greek.

As they ate, Angela was conscious of several eyes upon her. Niko stared at her hostilely, almost without pause, making her acutely uncomfortable. No wonder he resented her, believing she was a fortune hunter trying to ensnare Savvas! Angela flushed at the very idea. Savvas himself was smiling at her from across the table. Alex still wore dark glasses, so Angela couldn't tell if he noticed her or not. Stephanie was involved with the children, and so was Mrs. Pallas, although she kept switching her attention from them to Angela.

"Mother says to tell you how much she appreciated the kindness of your aunt in having my sister home with you during the holidays when she was at college with you," Savvas translated. "Mother hopes you are comfortable. You are to ask for anything you might wish, and you are to stay as long as you like. And if I may add my own wish—"

"That will do, Savvas," Alex warned his brother.

Savvas made a face but refrained from flirting with Angela for the rest of the meal.

Angela noticed that Petra, who consistently ignored her, was being particularly solicitous to old Mr. Pallas. He smiled and nodded and seemed quite taken with her.

For her part, Angela thought that Petra managed to make a spectacle of herself in every situation. She was loud and overly dramatic, and even when trying to be pleasant, she gave herself away with her extravagant gestures. She had a way of saying, "Please pass the salt," as if she were imparting a piece of important information that couldn't fail to impress. Petra, Angela felt, didn't care a damn for old Mr. Pallas. She was merely trying to get on his good side, and he was old enough to be flattered by the attentions of a beautiful young girl.

Whenever Petra tried to say something to the children, however, she was met with a total rebuff. To Petra's barely concealed rage, Miki and Crista kept calling things out in English to Angela and making laughing faces at her. The children really were very sweet, and Angela was growing fonder of them by the minute. Mrs. Pallas smiled shrewdly, seeming to take in everything happening at the table all at once.

Only Alex sat impassively, correcting his children when he felt they were growing too boisterous.

Angela was able to eat little, and her heart thumped nervously as she anticipated her impending interview with Alex. She had no doubt that he would do exactly as he pleased, in spite of what his sister or even his parents might think. Alex's parents treated him with deference, even as his attitude toward them was one of kindly, filial devotion.

Alex was the first to leave the table. Timorously Angela followed him with her eyes, until she noticed that Mrs. Pallas was watching her, and she guiltily lowered her head to her plate.

She had fifteen minutes before being called on the carpet, and to divert herself she asked Stephanie to show her the house.

It was truly beautiful, utterly unlike any place Angela had ever seen before. The different levels, the winding outdoor corridors, the many steps, the unexpected turnings, nooks, and crannies were confusing but charming. From the open windows the sweet fragrance of jasmine permeated everywhere.

The furnishings reflected the simple island life, quite different from the heavy brocade, crystal, and period antiques of the mansion in Athens. Here were ancient pottery, sculptures, and Byzantine icons considered priceless and not allowed to be taken out of Greece. There were exquisite hand-carved wooden door panels and screens showing peasant motifs, as well as old woven Cretan rugs in black, dark green, and muted red. All the furniture—functional and of simple lines—was hand-carved. Gaily painted plates were hung on the walls for decoration, and there were wooden and marble tables and chairs with woven rush seats.

"We live like islanders here," Stephanie told Angela happily. "Goat's milk for breakfast, and thick yogurt, fresh fruits and vegetables from the garden, and fish from the sea. Why are you looking at your watch?"

"Alex wants to speak to me in his study," Angela murmured.

"Oh? what would *you* possibly have done to deserve that dubious honor? I can remember all the reprimands from Alex in that same study when I was younger. Don't look so serious. I was only joking. Alex surely isn't going to lecture *you*."

As Angela passed through the door indicated by Stephanie, she was not so sure.

Alex was sitting at a large desk thumbing through papers. He did not look up when she entered the room.

She stood at the door awkwardly, her eyes taking in his blue shirt open at the collar, his regal head bent slightly over his work. She felt a shiver work its way down her backbone and she began to tremble. When he looked up at her suddenly, she caught her breath in agitation.

"Do you need an invitation to sit down when I am already seated?" he asked.

He spoke so scathingly that her apprehension shifted to annoyance. Who did he think he was to treat her so brutally? She perched stiffly in a chair in front of his desk, poised for the next onslaught.

"What do you think of this English test?" he asked her abruptly, shoving a thin red-bound book across the desk.

Angela was so astonished that she could only stare at him for a moment. Then she lowered here eyes and reached for the volume with trembling fingers. She had never met such an unpredictable man.

Angela tried to focus her eyes on the book, but she kept seeing Alex's darkly handsome face as it had appeared to her a moment before—the strong brows meeting over dark, intense eyes, the straight nose with the slightly flaring nostrils, the well-formed, expressive lips that so often mocked her.

The book was meant to teach English to Greek children. It had large type, with more illustrations than text. The pictures were gaily colored, showing animals on a farm.

"Oh, these are Stephanie's," Angela said impulsively, smiling at them in delight. "Aren't they simply wonderful—"

"Do you think the book would be appropriate to teach my children?" he interrupted briskly.

Angela expelled a sigh of relief when she finally realized that he hadn't called her in here to scold her at all but merely to ask her opinion. She turned the pages, reading quickly. "It's very simple, and wouldn't broaden their vocabulary beyond words used in the barnyard, but as a quick, elementary text, to be used in conjunction with something more comprehensive, it would be fine. The greatest value in this volume is the illustrations. They will attract a child's attention. However, Miki and Crista could learn everything in this book in one lesson."

"I see," Alex said, leaning back in his chair, his expression mocking. "That is the carefully considered opinion of the young lady with the obstinate pedagogic theories. Could *you* teach my children everything in this book in one lesson?"

"Of course," she replied without hesitation.

"Then I take up your challenge, Miss Blair. Stephanie said you would be making yourself useful in this respect during the course of this summer. After I see what you can do, I'll set your salary."

Angela flushed. He was talking to her as if she were merely an employee rather than Stephanie's guest.

"I think, Mr. Pallas, that under the circumstances, a token payment will be sufficient. I came here principally to spend time with Stephanie, not to accumulate drachmas. My lessons with your children will be largely informal and a great deal of fun for me, as I find them absolutely delightful. I don't view this as a job, exactly—"

Alex narrowed his eyes, and his mouth curved into a derisive smile. "You are willful, Miss Blair, and quite presumptuous. It is I who will decide what is to be done in my own house, not you. You have made a rash statement that you can impart the contents of this text to Miki and Crista in one lesson. Very well, then, we have a wager, and I will hold you to it. If you succeed, you have a job, and at a salary I and I alone will will determine. If you fail, you remain as a guest, and my children will come by their knowledge of English in some other manner."

How Angela's cheeks burned at his words. He was a very worldly man, skilled in repartee, while she was only an inexperienced girl from a small town. She had always been surrounded with kind friends and loving attention, and she was unprepared to deal with his rancorous attack. It both hurt and angered her.

Misinterpreting her silence as agreement, Alex said airily, "That will be all, Miss Blair."

Angela rose uncertainly to her feet. "I wonder, Mr. Pallas, if you have any texts that can be used as instruction about useful aspects of life, not only to teach the children English. UNESCO, I believe, puts out certain books that are helpful in showing children that differences in language, customs, and color of skin are not important—"

"Yes, yes," Alex said quickly, as if he hadn't the least interest. "The next time I am in Athens I will bring with me the books that I would like you to use."

78

Standing in front of him, Angela tried to contain her annoyance. Was he being deliberately obtuse or did he intend such rudeness? While she fully recognized that she should not risk angering him further, the thought of the children's welfare impelled her to speak out.

"What I mean, Mr. Pallas, is that the children have some strange ideas—"

"For example?" he challenged her.

"For example, when I asked Crista what a daughter was, she told me it was a girl son!"

Alex had the impudence to laugh in Angela's face. "That's charming. What's wrong with that? Most original, I think, Angela."

Ignoring the shiver down her back as he spoke her name, she said, "It—it implies that females have to take their very concept of existence from males—"

"Yes, quite," he agreed without apology. "In your country it is the other way around, but my daughter is Greek, after all, and will not, I hope, be forever chafing at her status, to the intense boredom of all who have to listen to her."

Angela was forced to bite back her retort, because she was so dangerously close to losing her temper with him that she feared her own reactions. Quickly lowering her angry eyes, she took a deep breath and tried to contain her wrath. Surely he didn't seriously believe what he was saying but was merely teasing her, trying to get a rise out of her—and succeeding admirably.

"I—I should tell you, Mr. Pallas, that I am not remaining for the entire summer, only for the month of July. I mean—you—you said the summer, and I wondered if Stephanie had told you—" She stopped, flustered, as he glared at her.

"Ah, yes." He rapped on the desk with a pen, pursing his lips mockingly. "I was forgetting your wedding.

79

You are marrying a lawyer, I believe? A childhood sweetheart? Or at least so Stephanie has informed me."

Angela's face turned fiery with distress. "No! I—I mean—plans have not actually been made. . . ." She swallowed painfully, feeling like an idiot standing there before him like a prisoner on trial.

"In any case," he murmured, a resentful expression clouding his features, "we will see the outcome of our little wager before making any final decisions. Well, my dear girl, hadn't you better begin?"

Angela felt her throat closing up. He had called her his "dear girl." Even as a figure of speech it so affected her that she could only nod under his mocking scrutiny.

He bent his head to his papers without a word more. She had been dismissed.

Chapter Six

Angela had no doubt that she could win the wager with Alex. She counted on the quick intelligence of the children, as well as on her "fun theory" of learning. In spite of her vulnerable financial position, she rashly decided to refuse any payment whatsoever for her teaching. It would be a labor of love for Miki and Crista.

When Angela emerged into the bright glare of the afternoon sun, partly protected by a large-brimmed straw hat, she found Savvas and Stephanie waiting with four donkeys. Miki and Crista were already mounted one behind the other on theirs and were shouting, "*Pame*, Angela, let's go."

"Ah, here's my beauty," Savvas said, kissing his hand to her. "Let me help you mount your donkey."

They began a slow trek, single file, down a path parallel to the sea. Angela, riding directly behind the children, decided to start her lesson. "This," she began, patting her animal on the neck, "is a donkey."

While the children parroted her words gleefully, she observed, in passing, the garden patch, and a little beyond, the orange and lemon grove. Behind it were the wonderful olive trees. Several of the island workers passed them, on their way home for the afternoon siesta. They stopped to greet Savvas and Stephanie, who shook each by the hand and called them all by name.

"*Sto kaló,*" they murmured, their smiles beamed at Angela.

She repeated the greeting, which meant, "May all things be good for you."

After riding halfway to the other tip of the island, they returned to the sandy beach where they had originally come ashore.

The sand was golden and fine, and there was a sprinkling of smooth white stones, some of them pure marble. Intrigued, Angela began collecting them, while the children shrieked and whooped, following her example.

From a small cabin among the evergreens Savvas removed flippers, snorkles, and a canvas raft.

In the water Angela, gently moving her flipper-clad feet, followed Stephanie beyond the beach and toward the rocks, peering through her mask. Angela found herself in a wonderful sea-covered forest. Flat fishes of different sizes, some with pastel stripes, some with spots, swam lazily past volanic rocks enrobed in richly patterned green seaweed. Jet-black, shiny sea urchins clung to the crevices, and Angela was warned against touching their sharp spines. She floated dreamily over the strange and marvelous underwater flora, which appeared to dance to the rhythm of the waves.

When the two girls emerged from the sea, they saw Savvas floating on the raft very close to shore. "This is the life," he announced as he blew a jet of water into the air like a geyser, sending the children into screams of laughter.

Angela took out the English picture book and began to look at the brightly colored illustrations. Stephanie had moved into the shade and was having a nap.

The children rushed to Angela's side, curious about

the book on her lap, and soon they were able to identify the animals and farm buildings that were illustrated. Angela took them through the book three times, certain that they had mastered it. After the lesson she encouraged them to lie down and rest under the trees.

Angela was about to do the same when she found Savvas beside her. "Lie on the raft. It is very soft and will keep the sand out of your beautiful eyes and the needles off your smooth back. And I will lie right beside you." He put his arm across her shoulders and kissed her cheek.

"Don't, Savvas. I can't sleep if you pester me."

"Pretend I am only a butterfly nestling on a flower."

As usula, Angela had to laugh at him.

He laughed in turn, showing his even white teeth in a jolly smile that dimpled his round face. "It is very clever, the way you are teaching Miki and Crista. You know, you have everything I could ever wish for in a wife. Beauty, intelligence—"

"Savvas, please stop—"

"Why? Why should I stop? Your boyfriend in America can't hear me. Besides, he has probably forgotten you already."

"What? With all my peerless traits?" she teased him. However, her smile hid a heavy heart. She was thinking that *she* had almost forgotten Rory. She was going to have to write him something, and soon. But what could she say? She was riddled with confusion. She wished she were able to confide in Stephanie as she used to, but she dared not express her doubts about Rory. Not yet, especially since Niko believed she was trying to capture Savvas. Besides, Niko's atrocious behavior had set up a barrier between her and Stephanie, and Angela didn't quite know what to do.

Angela fell into a troubled doze, dreaming that she

was running away from some danger in a pine forest and had become hopelessly lost. It was growing dark, and she was scared. Suddenly she tripped and fell onto the pine needles. They were sticking her sharply. A dark shadow fell over her and then she was grabbed in a man's arms and violently embraced as a hard mouth covered hers with kisses. "Alex," she murmured in her dream, "Alex."

When Angela opened her eyes, she saw that Savvas was bending over her, and he was laughing. "Angela-mou, you fell off the raft. Come, it is time to return to the house before my terrible brother comes looking for us."

That evening at dinner Angela was terribly conscious of Alex, as always, although their last interview had left her shaken. Still, her glance lingered upon him again and again, and she kept forcing herself to tear her eyes away from him. Perhaps it was his red silk shirt. Every time he moved Angela could see the rippling of his powerful muscles. . . .

"You will waste away to nothing, Angela, if you don't eat," Savvas commented, while Petra snorted in contempt and turned her attention to charming the elder Mr. Pallas.

After the meal, while the adults drank tiny cups of thick, fragrant Greek coffee on the patio, Angela took from her bag the picture book and opened it. Instantly Miki and Crista rushed to her side, clamoring to "read" it.

Angela started with the first page. As she pointed to each picture the children told her the English name. They were almost perfect, except for a momentary confusion between a goose and a duck.

"Bravo, Angela," cried Savvas.

"See how good she is, Alex?" Stephanie chimed in

excitedly. "I told you Angela was a brilliant teacher."

Angela smiled shyly and hugged the children, who had climbed into her lap. "It is easy when the pupils are so quick to learn," she murmured.

Angela finally stole a look at Alex. Her pulse raced madly when she saw that his face was lit up by a smile of fatherly pride that for one exquisite moment included her.

Mrs. Pallas was nodding with approval, while the children preened and giggled, loving being the center of attention.

Alex complimented them, but not effusively. Angela could see that he was determined not to spoil them with too much praise.

All through the children's performance Petra had contrived to keep Mr. Pallas from following their progress by talking to him nonstop.

Angela was suddenly aware of Mrs. Pallas's eyes on her. The woman nodded, as if satisfied, and several times muttered, *"Katalavéno,"* under her breath. It meant that she understood something, but what? Angela blushed and carefully avoided looking at Alex further.

It was becoming dark. Mrs. Pallas rose and took the unwilling children to bed. Stephanie, looking at Niko with adoration, whispered to him, and the two went off together.

Feeling uncomfortable, Angela slipped away while Petra and Alex stood conversing with Mr. Pallas. Savvas had vanished.

Angela made for the olive grove. She loved the shapes of the trees, silhouetted against the evening sky like leafy sculptures. Back and forth she walked, her arms folded in front of her. She needed to think, to organize her feelings.

She began to fear that she was becoming too much

involved with Crista and Miki, and they with her. When it came time for her to leave, what then? Children never really understood why adults went away. They simply felt deserted.

The more she thought of her situation, the more Angela felt she should leave the island, leave Greece, and go home, where she belonged. In spite of the excitement, her enchantment with everything, she was jumpy and watchful here, constantly subject to shocks and surprises. The plain fact was that she couldn't cope with any of the three men on the island. Niko's malevolent glances and menacing approaches filled her with terror. Although Savvas's flirtation could not be taken seriously—nor did she wish to do so—it was giving rise to unfounded speculation. As for Alex— just the thought of him had a physical effect upon her that she could scarcely comprehend. That she was attracted to him she knew beyond any doubt, but she excused her feeling in all sorts of ways. She feared him slightly, she respected him, and in some ways she even disliked him. Certainly he was different from anyone she had ever met. Perhaps she was simply intrigued by the unfamiliarity. In addition, he looked so much like her vision of Apollo that she was thrown a little off-balance.

But was that all? As a picture of Alex floated before her, his dark hair, the proud way he held his head, his red silk shirt and slim-fitting trousers, her breath quickened and the palms of her hands grew moist.

Stop it, she ordered herself. You are being foolish. You are nothing to him, less than nothing. An employee, to be ordered about. You are confusing this often unpleasant, terribly arbitrary mortal with the god of your story book. It is all in your imagination, and

you are behaving like a silly child. Alex loves Petra
. . . she repeated to herself.

Angela heard voices nearby and she pulled back
behind a tree just in time to remain unobserved. Alex
and Petra walked past her, hand in hand, almost as if
her thoughts had summoned them. Petra was speaking
rapid Greek, using her free hand for swift, imperious
gestures.

Angela couldn't see their faces because it had grown
too dark, but the closeness with which they walked
made her heart ache with an undefined longing. She
had never been of a jealous disposition, and surely it
was not jealousy that she felt now. Even if there had
been no Petra, Alex would have been far beyond her
reach. Besides, she certainly wouldn't want a man who
was so mercurial, so authoritarian, so—so—everything,
she thought, her heart sinking in despair.

As the couple passed from view Angela decided that
her uneasy feeling had to do with Petra in relation
not to Alex but to the children. Angela was certain
that Petra would make a terrible stepmother. There
was something cold about the woman, something de-
ceitful and possibly cruel. Petra might simply dislike
the children because they were the offspring of her
original rival. Why would Alex, a man of such sophis-
tication and discernment in so many ways, contemplate marrying a woman who was so obviously alien-
ated from his children, especially when he had rejected
her the first time?

Angela pondered the question as she resumed her
stroll among the olive trees. Did Alex simply wish to
please his old father by making a commercially ad-
vantageous marriage? But surely, with all the Pallas
wealth, another producer of paper, another printer,
could be found. Anyway, she doubted that a man like

Alex would be guided in such an important decision by an old man's stubbornness. Of course, the most obvious explanation—and the one that Angela cared for the least—was that Alex loved Petra. Perhaps he hadn't originally, but he surely must now. She certainly was a beauty, if one was not put off by her icy blue eyes, her dramatic gestures, her spiteful tongue—

"Oh!" Angela halted, petrified. She had walked straight into somebody and her terror was not diminished when she realized it was Niko, and that he had immediately taken hold of her arm.

"What are you dreaming that has made you blind in both eyes?" he asked her harshly. "Let me guess. You are thinking of the delights of this island, of how wonderful it would be to be mistress here, to be a Pallas and have as much money and comfort as you could possibly wish."

Angela shook his arm off and backed away. "That is a terrible accusation and entirely untrue. I know very well you don't like me, but for Stephanie's sake you might—"

"Leave Stephanie out of it. If you're thinking of going to her with stories, I can tell you that she'd never believe a word against me. However, I will not stand by and watch you flaunt yourself in front of Savvas and upset the boy with your tricks in the hope that he will lose his senses and make you an offer of marriage—"

Angela simply couldn't bear to listen to him, nor did she have the stamina to argue. She turned and ran through the trees toward the house. Her eyes filled with tears, and she began to sob as she fled. She was unaccustomed to being spoken to like this and had no weapons with which to defend herself. She knew only that Niko was mistaken, but she didn't see how she could prove it—unless she left the island without delay.

She stopped a short distance from the house to catch her breath and dry her eyes. Really, it would be sensible simply to go home now. Then she thought of Miki and Crista, smiling and happy, soon to be faced with a stepmother like Petra, and her heart ached for them. If she could remain here a little while longer . . .

A pair of arms encircled her, and she was roughly embraced by Niko. As she squirmed in panic he whispered in her ear, "Stop playacting and pretending to be a little innocent. Savvas is no match for you, but I am."

Angela pushed desperately against him. "Let go of me," she pleaded, struggling. Suddenly, as abruptly as Niko had grabbed her, he released her, curling his lip in savage contempt as she stumbled up the front steps.

She could hear voices coming from the patio. The others were relaxing, enjoying the cool breezes of the evening. Angela, however, wished only to go to bed and forget her troubles in sleep.

As she entered the house she almost bumped into Alex. Trying to avert her face as she slipped past him, Angela jumped in fright when he extended his arm against the wall in front of her, blocking her progress.

"Stop a moment. What's the matter? You look so frightened." He bent and scrutinized her. When she turned her face to the wall, he put his hand beneath her chin and forced her to look at him. Tears still clung to her thick eyelashes, and her face was flushed and unhappy.

"You've been running. And crying. Why, Angela?"

His voice was so soft, so concerned that she nearly burst into tears at such unexpected gentleness. As it was, his use of her first name sent such a thrill through her that she had to lean against the wall for support. "I—it's—nothing," she whispered hoarsely.

He didn't press her further for an explanation, but with his fingertip caressed her cheek for a moment. His cool touch on her hot skin was electrifying. She began to shake.

"I see you are upset. Come in here." Putting an arm around her trembling shoulders, Alex drew her into his study and led her to a chair. He seated himself opposite her, his eyes searching her face. Was it sympathy she saw there?

For a few moments they sat in silence. Angela breathed deeply and tried to compose herself. She must not break down further in front of Alex.

"Do you want to tell me what's wrong?" he asked at length.

She lowered her eyes silently.

Alex leaned forward suddenly, his body tense. "Is it Savvas? Has that brother of mine done something—"

"No, no, not at all," Angela hastily assured him. "I—I simply was out walking, thinking. It has nothing whatever to do with Savvas."

"I see." Alex, looking at her as if he did not believe her words, sat back in his chair, and she heard him sigh. Mercifully he changed the subject.

"I wanted to congratulate you on winning our wager. Also, I must apologize for doubting your word in connection with the teaching of my children. I see that you do not promise more than you are able to deliver. Miki and Crista have certainly taken to you. I have confidence now that after spending the summer with you, they will be speaking fluent English. As for your salary—"

"Please," Angela interrupted, flushing uncomfortably. "I want no salary. It will be my pleasure to teach them. Also, I am a guest in your house, and—"

90

"Rubbish! Nothing of the sort. You would be a guest even if you spoke no English, even if you were a Turk. You are Stephanie's dearest friend, and that is enough. Since you are so touchy about payment, I will write you a check for what I wish and mail it to your home. Now, let us say no more about the matter."

"But—but I must say something more, Mr. Pallas—"

He frowned and held up his hand to silence her. "Do you find me so old, so removed from your generation that you must address me as you do my father? Won't you call me Alex?"

A momentary flicker of hurt transformed his features, and Angela had the wild impulse to kiss his cheek. She clenched her fists and forced herself to say in an even tone, "Of course not, Alex."

He smiled wryly. "Thank you. You had started to say something before I made an issue of my name."

"Oh. Uh, yes. As I tried to tell you this afternoon, I'm not sure I can stay beyond the end of July. My younger sister is all alone at home and—and—" She stopped as the familiar glower turned Alex's face cold and angry.

"Yes, of course," he said, a bitter note creeping into his voice. "It doesn't occur to you that to start to teach the children and then to go away might do more harm than good. But then it is not of them you are thinking, but of your sister. *And* your fiancé, whom you are not honest enough to mention!"

Alex was talking himself into a cold fury. He jumped up and strode to the open window, his back to Angela.

"I don't wish to blackmail you, but if you cannot remain for the entire summer, I must ask you not to teach them at all."

"But—but I never intended to stay until the end of August," Angela cried, jumping up in turn. "I wrote

91

Stephanie that I would be coming only for July. And still you—you had agreed to the English lessons—"

"Yes, I did. You are correct." Alex turned and faced her. "But now I have changed my mind. You will be paid your salary regardless, since it is I who backed out of the arrangement you had apparently made with Stephanie—"

"No! I refuse! That is out of the question." Angela could not contain her agitation. "I will not accept a penny of payment, especially for work that I have not done. Furthermore—" She could not go on. Her voice broke and her eyes misted with tears, which began to roll down her cheeks. She dabbed at them furiously with her fingers, but still they came. Sobbing, she turned her back.

Alex had walked toward her and now stood directly behind her. "You believe I am wrong?"

Miserably Angela shook her head. "I think you are probably right," she sobbed. "It's just that I wanted to teach them."

"Yes, I do see that." He handed her a folded clean white handkerchief, which she made good use of, feeling like a silly child. She had never made such a fool of herself.

When she returned his handkerchief, he said softly, "We will say no more this evening. You think it over."

He walked with her to the door. "I hope you will decide to remain. In any case, let us have no hard feelings between us. *Kalinikhta*, Angela. Sleep well, my—sleep well." He bit his lip, nodded morosely, and shut the door in her face.

For a moment Angela stood rooted, a shiver going through her. How mercurial he was, how changeable. One minute here would be a closeness, a sympathy between them. In the next moment his abruptness and chilliness would make her feel as if she had been dropped into an icy pool.

When she regained her room, she fell across her bed, fully dressed, while her mind spun and her emotions churned painfully. What was she going to do?

Every reasoning part of her brain said emphatically, Leave. Leave now. Don't wait until the end of July. Write to Rory and say you have had enough of Greece and are coming home. Leave Savvas and Niko, and Alex. Especially Alex.

And yet, with all her heart she wanted to remain. She thought of the satisfaction she would derive from seeing Crista and Miki increase their vocabulary day by day. The island was so wonderful in every way. She loved the house, the beach, the olive trees, and the wonderful smell of the jasmine that was everywhere. She adored the extraordinary light for which Greece was famous, a heavenly light she had experienced nowhere else.

One thing was clear to Angela. Either she had to remain for the entire summer or leave immediately, even if it hurt Stephanie terribly. If she remained, it meant ending her engagement to Rory. In spite of the nasty insinuations Niko had made to her, he—and Savvas, for that matter—had sensed that her feelings for Rory were not what they should be. Even Alex had accused her of not being honest. There was some justification to his contention. She needed to be very honest with herself at the moment.

She was extremely fond of Rory, but did she love him the way a wife should love her husband, the way Stephanie appeared to love Niko? No, she did not. There was also her dangerous attraction to Alex. Surely if she had been in love with Rory, no other man—no matter how devastating and exciting—could have wrought such havoc with her emotions.

* * *

The following morning Stephanie suggested to Angela that they go by donkey to Rocky Point, at the other tip of the island. "We have hardly spent a moment alone, and today is our big opportunity, for my brothers and Niko are having a meeting with Papa."

Angela sighed with relief to think of some hours spent away from Alex.

Mounting their donkeys, the girls ambled lazily along the dusty path for four miles. Rocky Point was a narrow promontory jutting into the sea. The water was rougher and colder than in the protected bay at the beach, but the rock formations were spectacular, and snorkling was even more exciting. Angela imagined that the rocks were the remains of an island that had once been submerged by the sea, like the legendary Atlantis.

The girls swam, had a water fight, and went in a fruitless pursuit of a lizard, which looked like a prehistoric dinosaur in miniature. They wanted to examine it more closely, but it was too quick for them and scurried out of sight into a crevice.

The two friends finally sank down, exhausted. Stephanie, raising herself on one elbow after a few minutes, looked at Angela curiously. "I've been waiting and waiting for you to tell me, but you haven't."

"Tell you what?" Angela pretended ignorance, but she suspected what was coming.

"Tell me what's going on. Your conference with Alex, for example. My parents, by the way, like you a lot. Papa doesn't say much, of course, and with Petra coiled around his neck like a snake he can hardly breathe. But Mother is enchanted by you; she said so. She seems to have some secret happiness, but she won't tell me another thing. Alex and Mother are a lot alike. Both of them are positive people, and they must have their own way or else. Papa, Savvas, and I are more similar to each other. We can be turned from our course by persuasion. Anyway, it's fortunate that Alex and Mother usually agree."

Angela flushed. That might be, but surely they were not in agreement in their opinion of her.

"You still haven't answered me, Ange. What is it? I used to be your best friend," Stephanie said, pouting.

"Still are and always will be," Angela assured her, contrite, and giving her a hug. She paused. "Alex was talking to me about the English lessons for the children. You see, he has asked me to remain for the whole summer—"

"Hooray!" shouted Stephanie. "That's more like it. He has been behaving in such a peculiar manner since you arrived. Anyway, that's simply wonderful—"

"Shh. Not so fast. It isn't that simple," Angela interrupted, sighing. "You remember I agreed to come only for a month. Alex agreed, too, but now he has changed his mind. He thinks it would be bad for the children if I left at the end of July, in the middle of their lessons. In fact, he won't let me even start the lessons unless I agree to the whole summer."

"But that's perfect! You know how much we all want you, Ange, for as long as possible. Oh, I wish you could stay forever!"

"Steph, I—I can't, because if I stay longer than originally planned, I'll have to tell Rory—"

"Let Rory come here and spend August with us! No wonder you've been moping, my poor Angela. I've been so selfish and thoughtless. We would be thrilled to have Rory with us, and I'll write him a note myself—"

"No, don't!" Angela shouted in alarm. "I—I mean—"

Stephanie's eyes grew rounder. "What's the matter?"

"Oh, Steph, I don't want Rory to come here at all!"

Angela hadn't realized she was going to say the words until they were out. "I've been having second thoughts about—about our engagement."

"Oh, Ange! Oh, dear, I begin to see." Stephanie was silent for a few moments. "Is it since—since coming here?"

Angela stubbornly kept her head down, running her finger over a smooth rock beside her. Her face and ears were burning, and she knew that her color had deepened. Was it so obvious, then?

Stephanie sighed, and said gently, "It's not that I wouldn't adore to have you in our family, truly, Ange. But you know—oh, how shall I say it? Savvas is not in a position to take a wife, especially if Mother and Alex opposed it. Savvas is old enough, certainly, but he's still studying. It's his own fault. He could be independent, working in the business by now. The truth is that Savvas has come to us with a different girl every few months. But Alex will never let Savvas marry until he shows some responsibility in the business."

Angela slowly exhaled, her color returning to normal. Really, she was being incredibly stupid. Of course it would never have crossed Stephanie's mind to connect her with Alex.

"My feelings have nothing whatever to do with Savvas," Angela said with perfect conviction. "This is only between us, Steph. You mustn't mention a word. The fact of the matter is that, although I'm fond of Rory, I'm not sure I'm in love with him. When I watch you, with Niko . . ." And Petra with Alex, she was thinking, but couldn't bring herself to say so.

Stephanie put her arm around Angela and hugged her with compassion. "Forgive me, Ange, for being such an imbecile. You came to Greece to have some time to yourself, to decide what to do. But Rory loves you, of course—"

Angela turned her violet-blue gaze upon her friend. "Does he truly, Steph? I mean, isn't it mostly a case of propinquity? Childhood sweethearts, everyone expecting us to marry, and so forth? Everything taken for granted, calm, unflurried, without excitement?"

"Yes, that's true. But that's so—forgive me—American. We Greeks cannot do anything without flurry or excitement. We feel everything so strongly, and show our feelings so openly."

Angela was silent. Behavior was one thing, feelings another. Surely nobody felt more strongly than she did —about some things.

"If you have doubts about Rory, you must certainly give yourself more time. Oh, Angela, you are the most beautiful girl I know. And you've led such a protected life. Goodness, the way all the men looked at you that night at the Lampari's party! You could have any man in the whole world. If you decide against—well, getting married—you could stay in Greece and work for us. And travel with us."

Stephanie's velvety eyes grew thoughtful. "We never talked of love much at college. There was too much else going on, and I never was serious about the boys I dated. But I can tell you this: Even though I know Niko loves me and that we will be married within a few months, every time I see him my heart beats madly so that I think it's going to burst. I want to spend every minute with him that I can. I see his faults, of course, and we argue often. He is pigheaded, jealous, and terribly prejudiced. And yet I wouldn't change a hair on his head. I love him even more for his imperfections—"

Angela blanched as her friend spoke, aware of yet another "imperfection" in Stephanie's precious Niko. What would Stephanie say if she knew how Niko had been tormenting Angela?

"You're miles away, Ange, so I won't say another word or ask any more questions. I make you a promise, though. You can count on me for anything. You can come and live here and be my sister, truly. I have felt from the moment we met that there was something between us that transcends all barriers. I remember how shy and uncomfortable I was, knowing hardly any English, and how you took me home to stay with your aunt and your sister. A Greek never forgets a kindness, true, but it is more than that in this case. I'm ashamed to say that I almost hope that you do decide to stay in Greece with us for selfish reasons. Because then we could be as we once were, instead of having to write silly letters."

Angela was deeply touched by her friend's affection. "I love you too, Steph. Nobody has ever been dearer. And now, let's have a swim."

Angela dived into the water, assailed by guilt for not having told the complete truth to Stephanie. How would her friend react if she knew that Angela feared she was falling in love with Alex?

Chapter Seven

Later that afternoon Angela stood at the window of
her room, looking down at the beach. Savvas, Niko,
and Alex were near the water. The *Crysula* had been
hauled onto a cradle by some workmen, and the three
men were scraping and caulking her. For once Angela
was able to stare at Alex without restraint. He was
the tallest and, to her, the most magnificent of the
three. His broad shoulders narrowed to a slim waist
and hips, and she could see his strong, hard muscles
glistening in the sun. He gave the orders. She could
faintly hear his confident voice instructing the other
two, his tone gathering mockery when he addressed
the playful Savvas.

Angela had meant to take the children to the beach
for an afternoon swim while their grandparents rested
and Stephanie did some book illustrations. However,
the prospect of being scrutinized by the three men on
the beach made her hesitate. Might it not be better to
take the children to Rocky Point? They would have
more fun off by themselves.

When Angela had collected the children and they
were mounting their donkeys, she noticed Petra in the
back doorway, watching them. Angela hesitated, wondering if she ought to invite Petra to join them. What
discouraged her from speaking was the cold, unsmiling
face the other woman presented.

The three had a wonderful afternoon at Rocky Point. The children had been coming to the island every summer, and there seemed to be no habitable corner of the place they didn't know intimately. Miki showed Angela a shallow pool containing inch-long crabs that nipped at their toes so gently, she felt as if she were being tickled by a feather. Crista knew where on the hills to gather wild thyme and sage to take home to Maria for the kitchen. Angela asked the children the Greek words for things, and they giggled with amusement at being able to teach their teacher.

When the children grew tired of scampering all over, they snuggled into Angela's arms for a rest. Holding one on each side, Angela allowed her thoughts to float aimlessly. She closed her eyes for a few moments.

At least that was what she had thought. When she opened them and looked at her watch, she saw, incredulously, that she'd been asleep for more than an hour. The children were nowhere to be seen.

"Miki, Crista! Time to go home," she called.

There was no answer. Angela rose to her feet and began to look for them. They weren't near the rocks—and, in fact, she'd warned them to be very careful. They weren't playing on the hillside among the wild herbs, nor were they in the meadow behind the hills.

Her heart beginning to pound in fear, Angela looked down into the water. She could see nothing there, but the sea now seemed quite choppy and the waves were crashing heavily against the rocks, sending up jets of white-capped, salty spray.

Frantically Angela ran to the donkeys. The two animals, still tethered, were calmly grazing, so the children hadn't ridden away. Probably it was silly of her to be so worried. They were on their own island, after all, and everyone there was a friend. One of the workmen, in fact, might have spotted them and taken them home.

But what about the churning water? If someone were to fall into the sea and hit his head against a rock . . . Angela had to force herself to stop thinking along such lines. The most obvious explanation was that the children had wandered off and were perfectly all right

Still, Angela kept having the nagging thought that they wouldn't have gone so far from her that they wouldn't hear her call them. She was a light sleeper. Surely she would have heard them playing nearby. They were not children who could vanish without a sound.

Angela cried their names until her voice was strained. Then she mounted her donkey and tied the children's animal behind to follow. Perhaps she would meet Crista and Miki on the road.

Angela rode as fast as she could prod her donkey to go, but every moment caused her worry to increase. Once she thought she heard their voices, but it turned out to be only the cries of some shrill little birds.

Angela rode all the way home without catching sight of them, and by then she was frantic. She jumped off the donkey and rushed into the house, opening doors at random. She even peeked into the room shared by Mr. and Mrs. Pallas, who were still asleep and didn't hear her.

The house was silent. Angela knocked lightly on Petra's door, but got no response. When Angela boldly opened her door, she saw that the room was empty.

Rushing to her own room, Angela washed her face in cold water, trying to think calmly about what to do next. The three men were still working on the boat down at the beach. When she anticipated Alex's reaction to the disappearance of his children, Angela felt sick. Should she awaken Stephanie and let her break the news to Alex? No, Angela must not be so cowardly. She had been responsible for the children, and she would have to tell Alex herself. There wasn't a moment to lose.

Angela ran down to the beach. Not until Savvas looked up and began to whistle at her did she realize that she was still in her bikini.

"Alex, I must speak to you," Angela cried, without preliminaries. "I was at Rocky Point with the children, and I fell asleep—"

His face went white. "They're missing? Since when?" He dug his fingers into her arm until she gasped from the pressure.

Alex spoke rapidly in Greek to Niko, who glared at Angela as if she were a murderess. Mumbling under his breath, Niko ran in a different direction from Alex.

Only Savvas was sympathetic to her. "Never mind, Angela, we'll find them. They have to be somewhere. You know how children are, always wandering off. Did you look in the cave?"

"No, I don't know of any cave."

"Ah, you see? That's where they are, I'll stake my life on it. Alécco!" he yelled to his brother, who waved his hand impatiently. Alex hastily mounted a horse brought by a workman from the stable. In the next moment he was galloping toward Rocky Point.

Even through her misery and concern Angela couldn't help noticing how gracefully Alex rode, his strong thighs hugging the saddle.

Niko organized the others into search parties of two each, swearing in Greek when Savvas insisted upon pairing off with Angela.

"We'll go across the island this way, past the orange grove," Savvas told Angela confidently. "Who knows.

They may be playing ball with some oranges. As for the cave, Alex will look there first."

Angela meekly followed Savvas, yelling, "Crista, Miki," until she had no voice left.

An hour later they headed back to the house.

"Don't worry so, Angelamou; they're surely found by now. They may have gone into Stephanie's room and crawled under the bed and fallen asleep. The little monkeys, you can never tell what they're going to do next."

But the children were not in the house, nor had they been found. Alex was still searching, and Stephanie had joined in the general alarm. Without frightening her parents with the truth, Stephanie went to their room on a pretext. The children were not there.

When Alex rode into view on his horse, without the children, they all realized just how serious the situation was.

It was only when Angela asked if Petra had returned that Stephanie looked up with a glint in her eyes. "I wouldn't put it past her," she murmured. "Now that you mention it, she was missing from her room; it's the most likely possibility that she took them somewhere. She's been jealous of you ever since you arrived—"

"But surely nobody could deliberately do such a thing—"

"Oh, Petra could. She's very calculating. The children like you better, and she knows it. She may think if she gives Alex a fright, he won't let you spend so much time with the—Oh, look. Look, Angela, there they are!"

Petra came out of the orange grove, leading a child by each hand. Both were crying and rubbing their eyes. They looked dirty and worn out.

Alex jumped off his horse, and in a moment was embracing both of them tightly.

Angela felt her eyes stinging with tears of relief, while Stephanie looked wise and nodded, her theory supported by Petra's presence.

To the others, however, Petra was a heroine. Niko made a special point of praising her in loud English, which Angela knew was for her benefit.

A smug smile playing in the corners of her mouth, Petra imperiously swept the children from Alex and pulled them off to be bathed by Maria. Crista began to cry, while Miki turned his head to give Angela a mournful look, but she could only stand there miserably and let them be taken.

Suddenly Niko put his hand on Angela's elbow. "You see what comes of meddling," he hissed at her. "A Greek family is not like any other. I give you warning. Spend your time with Stephanie and don't stir up trouble. Otherwise it will end badly."

Angela stood alone in front of the house, feeling hot with shame and misery. Niko was right; certainly she had caused trouble. Idly she reached out and plucked a sprig of jasmine, holding it to her nose and breathing in the heavy, sweet aroma, which somehow increased the aching in her heart.

She had been careless and stupid, allowing Petra to get the better of her. Now surely she would have to leave. If, as seemed probable, she would not be permitted to have anything more to do with the children, there was little point in remaining. She didn't want to cause conflict between Niko and Stephanie. As for Alex . . .

Angela walked quickly past the house and into the olive grove. Only there did a sense of calm overtake her. There was an ageless, wise quality about the gnarled olive trees with their silvery leaves. Olive trees

104

were sturdy and enduring, which was why they thrived in the harsh Greek landscape.

Angela leaned her arms against the knotted trunk of an olive tree, putting her head down on her arm and remaining motionless for some moments. She was reminded of her childhood, when she had played hide-and-seek.

"Angela," said a voice behind her, sending an apprehensive chill down the length of her spine. Whirling guiltily, she faced Alex, wondering how long he'd been observing her.

"I'm not surprised you wish to hide your head," he said sternly. "Quite frankly, Angela, I am disappointed in you. No," he continued, waving his arm at her just as she had opened her lips to speak, "don't bother to defend yourself. That will make it even worse."

"I wasn't going to," she whispered. "I agree with you. I am disappointed in myself. I have no excuse. All I can offer is my most sincere regrets for all the trouble caused by my carelessness. I didn't expect Crista and Miki to wander away—"

"Oh, is that it! The pedagogic theories are about to undergo a reevaluation?" Alex asked derisively. "I do not appreciate that you are using my children as guinea pigs!"

"I'm not!" she cried, flushing with anger that he could even think such a thing. "I have admitted it was my fault. What was I to do, tie them up like animals? I—I hadn't planned to fall asleep—"

"You are missing the point, Miss Blair," he said icily, his formal address making her cringe. "Petra found my children wandering in the road, crying, bruised, and filthy. They had tried to climb down the rocks to reach the water. Just thinking of the danger makes me feel weak. They tried to wake you and couldn't, and became hysterical with fear. Of all

105

the places to take them by yourself, Rocky Point is the most ill-advised. If they had been on the beach, someone could have kept an eye upon them. Even Stephanie has never dared to take them to Rocky Point without another adult, preferably male," he said scornfully. "If you and Stephanie are foolish enough to risk danger by swimming off Rocky Point, that is bad enough. But for you to take it upon yourself to go there with my children, I consider totally irresponsible. You are proud and willful, Miss Blair. Those are, I believe, dangerous traits in a young woman. I assumed you had a larger measure of common sense, or I would never have let you anywhere near my children."

Alex's words stung her cruelly. "You speak as if I deliberately put the children in danger to test a pedagogic principle, as you call it. All I had in mind, I assure you, was a peaceful, lovely afternoon by ourselves. And we had that, for a while. It doesn't help to insult me because I made a mistake, which I have already admitted." Angela faced Alex, her eyes blazing. "Things will be easier all around, I think, if I just pack my bags and leave tomorrow by boat, plane, or any vehicle you care to put at my disposal!"

"What! It is *you* who are angry with *me*? How do you dare!" He moved closer to her, and she could see a muscle in his cheek twitching.

Angela stood her ground. "Of course I'm angry that you could even imagine that I would put the children at risk for a theory! I couldn't bear it if any harm came to Crista and Miki—" Angela's voice broke then, as she remembered her frantic worry, and she stifled a sob.

"You misunderstand me. I don't say you aren't fond of the children, only that your falling asleep was not the cause of the trouble. It was your unilateral action.

106

Was I in Timbuktu? Why not ask me where to take them swimming? Why not allow for your own fallibility? You are a stranger here and should have had the modesty to consult someone who has a better idea of the dangers to be encountered. Pride and willfulness, I repeat, are your faults, and a conceit that you know better than anyone else. Well, you don't, Miss Blair, as this afternoon has proved. I expect you to defer to my judgment in future."

Angela remained silent, trembling with conflicting emotions. He kept one hand in his pocket, the other tensely at his side, his fist clenching and unclenching. His dark eyes glowered at her, and she thought it was only by exercising tremendous control that he avoided striking her.

He was, she knew, waiting for her to surrender, to agree that he knew best in all circumstances. And because she couldn't do that, because she was used to exercising independent judgment, she stood stubbornly mute.

Besides, she was thinking along different lines. How did Petra happen to be so near Rocky Point? How could the children have failed to awaken Angela when she was such a light sleeper? Even more curious, why had the children gone with Petra in the first place when they loathed her?

Apparently Petra was quite good at making explanations to Alex that he accepted. Well, he might be blinded by love, but Angela was not. She was determined to find out from the children what had really happened.

Alex continued to stare at Angela, but his angry expression gradually faded. Although his eyes were still hard, they reflected something else she couldn't quite fathom.

Finally Angela said grudgingly, "I concede that I

107

was foolish to go to Rocky Point, and that I hadn't appreciated the danger, but not that I am willful and proud, and all that other stuff. Under the circumstances, however, it will be best if I leave the island as soon as possible." She spoke softly but firmly, yet couldn't help a small sigh.

For a moment they looked at each other in silence. Her heart beat quickly while she waited for his response. It seemed to be a long time in coming.

"Let us go back a bit before the angry words, Angela. Perhaps we both said too much in the heat of the moment. You have apologized, and I accept your apology. I want no more talk of your leaving. It means a great deal to my sister to have you here. And my mother wishes to repay the hospitality your family offered to Stephanie."

Angela disliked the turn of the conversation, and she flushed. He acted as if the only reason she was wanted at all was to repay an obligation. Before she could say anything, he spoke once more.

"I'm still waiting for your answer regarding the possiblity of remaining through August. In spite of our differences I believe that you are, on the whole, good for my children, and that you will teach them very well. They're normally quite happy to be with you. Tell me, Angela, what you wish to do." Alex's voice had grown huskier with his last few words.

I wish to fling myself shamelessly into your arms, she thought, flushing deeply.

Her longing for him was so acute that she turned her back so as not to reveal anything further. She feared she had already shown him too much. "I—I'm very tired now. I can't think. If you could possibly give me a little more time to consider—"

"As you wish," Alex said stiffly.

108

When she turned again, she saw that he had vanished.

Angela couldn't face dinner, so pleading a headache as an excuse, which was the truth, she had her meal brought to her room.

Stephanie insisted upon joining her for coffee, and Miki and Crista were at her heels. "How is your headache?" Stephanie asked with concern. "I can tell you that Petra will have more than that wrong with her when I get finished. She has absolutely brainwashed these two. I've done everything but shake them to get the truth out of them." Stephanie's eyes flashed with unaccustomed anger as she flopped at the foot of Angela's bed.

Angela heard her words only in a daze. She was too busy hugging the children. They had jumped into her arms and were giving her such sweet kisses that she quite forgot everything else.

"Petra is out to get you, Angela. Savvas agrees with me. I just told Alex exactly what I think. Men. They believe what they want to believe. Petra could do nothing with Alex for years, and now . . . Of course, her pride was hurt when he married Caterina, and Petra has recently redoubled her efforts. She'll stop at nothing to get him. I never used to care one way or another, but now my eyes have been opened. I told Alex so, and Savvas did, too, but he has decided not to hear one word against Petra and simply closes his ears."

Such is the consequence of love, Angela thought sadly. Would Stephanie, she wondered, listen to anything against Niko?

"I can imagine what Alex must have said to you before dinner, my poor Angela," Stephanie told her sympathetically.

With the children nestling comfortably in her arms, Angela was feeling much better. "Forget it, Steph. Alex was right in expecting me to check with him before taking the children far from home. He wants me to do so in future—"

Stephanie's face lit up. "Then you're staying for the summer?"

Before Angela could answer, a sharp rap sounded on the door. "Stephanie, I want you," Niko called.

"Story time," Angela told the children after Stephanie's departure. "Once upon a time, there was a brother and sister called Hansel and Gretel, who lived in a beautiful forest. . . ." Angela went on with the story, making some deliberate changes. She implied that the children had gotten lost because they followed a beautiful lady into the forest.

"She had a kitten," Crista suddenly said. "Petra had a kitten called Tutu. She said if we didn't tell, she would let us keep him. Oh, he's all white and so pretty. . . ."

Between the mixture of Greek and English, and with many gestures, Angela was able to piece together the truth. Petra had deliberately enticed the children from Rocky Point by means of a kitten, forbidding them to tell or she would take the kitten away forever. Even as they blurted out the truth they were fearful of the consequences.

Angela kissed them and assured them that she would tell nobody, not a soul. Petra was keeping the kitten in her room, and only if the children were nice to her would she let them see it.

It was time for them to go to bed. Angela kissed them good night and gave them over to Maria. Then, setting off for a walk, she thought how contemptible Petra was for frightening the children in that way.

Angela avoided the olive grove, fearing to meet Alex again, and went instead down to the beach. It was a still night with a full moon high in the sky. Removing her sandals, Angela walked at the water's edge. The wet sand felt cool under her feet, and she liked the way the foamy water gently lapped at her toes.

"Angelamou, here you are," exclaimed Savvas, hailing her from farther down the beach. "Wait, I will come with you."

Angela would have preferred to be alone but she felt she ought to thank Savvas for his support earlier in the day. He, at least, had not blamed her for the children's disappearance.

"Angela, if I had my rightful place in this family, I would soon show that arrogant brother of mine what a viper he has in his pocket! Stephanie and I were discussing it. That Petra, she is a menace. Alex thinks because he's thirty years old he knows everything. He tells us what's what, dispensing what he thinks is wisdom, like an ancient god."

Angela immediately thought of Apollo, and her heart contracted.

"Did the children tell you anything, Angela? I'm sure they're hiding something."

Angela kept silent. There was no point in revealing their secret to Savvas. He would tell Stephanie, and she would confront Petra. It was the children who would suffer in the end, and they would never forgive Angela for having told. The point was that if Alex wanted to believe Petra, he would do so, regardless of the evidence.

"Don't be sad, my little Angela. The children love you best, I know they do. Who could help it?" He put his arm around her.

111

"Please don't, Savvas," Angela said petulantly, pushing him away more roughly than she intended. "I'm tired and I'd like to go back now."

For once Savvas did not insist, though he looked at her reflectively. Silently they walked side by side. At the door of the house Angela gave him a peck on the cheek to say good night. He was a dear, sweet young man, and it wasn't his fault that she was feeling wretched.

It wasn't anybody's fault that she had been foolish enough to fall in love with Alex Pallas.

She had been trying to keep her feelings beneath the surface, but they had erupted finally and forced her to recognize their existence. Every day that she remained on the island was bound to make her more miserable. Could she agree to stay here for two months and torture herself with her hopeless love? Or should she go as soon as possible, back to her uncomplicated existence in Springport, and forget she'd ever set eyes on Alex Pallas?

Angela sat up half the night looking at the moon from her window and trying to come to some decision.

Four days later a letter came from home that helped her to make up her mind.

Chapter Eight

The letter was from Nancy, and Angela found it by
her plate at breakfast. Hastily she stuffed it into her
pocket, to read later in private. Two days previously
Alex and Niko had traveled by private helicopter to
Athens, and Angela had been greatly relieved by their
absence. She had seen a lot of Stephanie and the children and had enjoyed herself very much. Savvas was
insisting upon giving Angela Greek lessons, and she allowed it, to take her mind off her troubles.

Mrs. Pallas had taken to conversing with her as best
she could, and Angela was pleased. There was a
warmth about Mrs. Pallas, coupled with a purposeful
intensity, that reminded her of Alex. An unworldly
but highly intelligent woman, she seemed most curious
about Angela's background. Although Stephanie surely had been pumped for information, Mrs. Pallas apparently wanted to hear things directly from Angela.
She tried to answer the questions, stumbling over her
Greek, while the older woman smiled and patiently
corrected her.

This morning Angela excused herself from breakfast hurriedly and went to her room to read Nancy's
letter.

> You must be having a fine time, Angie, judging
> from the one postcard you sent me from Athens.

And only a postcard to Rory! He hasn't, of course, said a word against you, but I'm sure he's feeling bad that you haven't written him even one letter. We went to the movies Saturday night, and all I can say is that if you don't care enough to keep watch over what you have, somebody else may be only too willing to pay him the attention he deserves.

Angela grew warm as a pang of guilt stole over her. Of course Nancy was absolutely justified. Angela had no right to keep Rory on a string. Why then, did she hesitate to write and call it off? What was she waiting for? For her infatuation for Alex to end? How she wished it would! Perhaps her feelings would cool if she had the courage to pick herself up and go home. That was the best solution to her problems. Yet every time she looked at Miki and Crista, she wavered. In spite of their father's love for them and the devotion of Savvas and Stephanie—not to mention the blind adoration of the grandparents—Angela believed that they very much needed her at the moment. Someone had to counter Petra's hypocritical maneuverings. No child was a match for a scheming woman like Petra. If only Alex would come to see her for what she was, before it was too late.

Rereading Nancy's letter, Angela suddenly realized with a shock that Nancy might herself be in love with Rory. Certainly her sister had more in common with him than she did.

Angela went down to the beach and reclined on a mat, loving the warmth of the morning sun. She was mulling over Nancy's letter when Stephanie appeared.

"However long you decide to remain here, Ange, you simply must return in October and be my maid of honor. I couldn't have anyone else. Just say yes, with

114

no buts or anything," Stephanie demanded, her eyes suddenly very bright and round.

Angela recognized Stephanie's expression as indicating great sensitivity on the subject, so she smiled and said yes without qualification. October was a long time away.

"I still mean to find out what really happened with Petra and the children the day they were missing," Stephanie declared. "They might have been killed because of Petra. I know Papa wants a family connection with Leonidas, but poor Papa is way behind the times. He doesn't really understand that Alex has diversified so much that we don't need any old paper plant. If Petra were just anybody, it wouldn't matter. But because Alex turned Petra down that first time, Papa and Mother, too, I suppose, think the family owes her something."

"What actually happened?" Angela asked after a moment.

"Didn't I ever tell you? The Pallas family and the Leonidas family arranged the marriage. I was just a kid, but I remember Petra as beautiful and pleasant. Of course, I didn't know her well. Anyway, maybe she was in those days. We couldn't understand why Alex refused. He caused a terrible family crisis by going against Papa's wishes. Even Mother was furious, and usually she thinks Alex can do no wrong."

Angela chose her words carefully. "It's too bad that Alex's alternative to Petra didn't turn out to be satisfactory, especially for the sake of the children."

She sat up on her towel and hugged her knees with her arms. "Yes," said Stephanie, sighing, "it was a terrible thing for us all. Alex is very determined and strong in his opinions, just like Mother. Only because she is an old-fashioned woman she makes her wishes known in certain subtle ways that usually win Papa over. Alex doesn't have to tread on eggshells. When he realized that Papa expected him to marry Petra, he rebelled totally. The family didn't know if Alex simply didn't care for Petra or was bothered by the idea of an arranged marriage.

"There was to be a big engagement party," Stephanie continued, "and Alex had stormed out of the house and vanished for three days. The family was confident that he would return and do his duty, for such rebellion was unheard of in a prominent Greek family. However, the night of the party, he had arrived with a girl nobody had ever set eyes on before, saying she was his wife. There had been a violent scene. Alex and Papa had had such an argument that they nearly came to blows. Mama hadn't spoken to Alex for months, and the family only became reconciled when Miki was born."

Angela picked up a handful of golden sand and let it trickle through her fingers. "Was she very beautiful?"

"Caterina? Oh, she was quite attractive in her way, and not really a bad sort, but very high strung. Alex hardly knew her himself. He married her out of spite, I think, though in the beginning he tried to care for her. Caterina wanted to be an actress, and Alex was willing, within limits. I imagine he strikes you as the most impossible male chauvinist, but his bark is much worse than his bite. I believe he likes a woman of spirit and not just a passive creature. Just think how he puts up with Petra now.

"Anyway, unfortunately Caterina had no talent for anything but hysterics. When the children came along, she was irritated at the bother. That's when the marriage broke to pieces, with Alex and Caterina fighting all the time. It's a good thing Crista and Miki were too young to remember. I only saw what was happen-

116

ing when I came home on vacation. It was unpleasant, I can tell you. That was when Alex began to be so bitter. Maria had to take care of the children, especially after Caterina began to drink secretly. It was no secret to Alex, of course, and he was trying to get her to agree to medical treatment but she refused. Poor Caterina, I can feel sorry for her now. She probably suffered when she realized that Alex didn't really love her and saw that he had made a mistake. Anyway, one night she took the car. She was drunk, of course, and she drove like a madwoman all the way to Falirón until she lost control and crashed into a wall. Mercifully for her, it was all over instantly."

"How horrible." Angela shuddered, thinking of what they all must have suffered, perhaps Alex most of all, knowing that he had brought disgrace upon his family. She wondered for the hundredth time how he could even think of making another serious mistake with Petra.

"Poor Alex has been unlucky in love," Stephanie said, voicing Angela's opinion. "Petra will be bad for the children, but I can't do anything with him. He seems determined to marry her this time."

Stephanie gazed out at the water. "I must go now. Niko is giving me a sailing lesson. If you'd like to come along . . ."

Angela politely declined, while her heart began to beat a nervous tattoo against her ribs. If Niko was back, so, probably, was Alex.

But Alex was not at lunch, and neither was Petra.

"They've gone to Athens for the trousseau," Niko announced smugly, his eyes glinting with malevolence when he noticed Angela staring at Alex's empty chair.

She pushed the food around her plate miserably and put very little into her mouth, knowing it would hardly get past the lump in her throat.

The children seemed to be acting up more than usual, taking advantage of their father's absence. When a rooster began to crow—as they did at all hours on the island—Crista did a quite good imitation. Miki, who had just put a little meatball into his mouth, tried to swallow quickly in order to give his rendition. Suddenly he began to choke.

Mrs. Pallas screamed for help as Savvas banged Miki on the back, while Stephanie sought to put her fingers down his throat.

Angela jumped up and ran to Miki's side. "I know what to do," she shouted. She grabbed Miki and moved behind him, clasping her arms tightly around his stomach. When she brought her fists up sharply just under the rib cage, his mouth flew open and the meatball popped out like a cork from a champagne bottle.

While the boy recovered his breath, the whole family surrounded Angela and fell upon her with cries and kisses. Mrs. Pallas spoke to Angela rapidly in Greek, her voice breaking with emotion, while Savvas translated. Angela had saved Miki's life, and for that the family vowed eternal gratitude. Even Mr. Pallas, who had been very shy with Angela up to now, echoed his wife's words, holding her hands in his for a long while.

Angela was embarrassed by such effusiveness, murmuring shyly that all teachers of small children knew first aid.

"It's too bad Alex wasn't here to see this," Stephanie whispered to Angela after everyone had calmed down. "But he'll hear all about it, and so will Petra. She'll be purple with jealousy."

Not if she has been buying her trousseau, Angela thought with a pang.

In the evening, when they were all sitting over coffee, two children of the island workers shyly approached Angela and handed her a wreath woven from jasmine.

"It is a custom of the island, for visitors," Mrs. Pallas told her slowly in Greek.

"And one worthy of a goddess like you," said Savvas. "That's what they take you for, with your blond hair. Come, Angela, we must go for a walk. You must be seen wearing your crown," he beseeched her, putting it on her head.

Angela saw Mrs. Pallas frown and say something to Savvas, but he merely kissed his hand at his mother and insisted upon dragging Angela away. "You are the most perfect girl in the world. I will not rest until you tell me that you prefer me to that lawyer across the sea, who lets you out of his sight for the summer. I wouldn't for a minute if you were mine."

"Don't, Savvas," Angela said, pained. She seemed to think of Rory only when somebody else mentioned him first.

Savvas became more affectionate, finally halting and trying to embrace her. He held her so tightly for a moment that she couldn't move or even breathe. "Please, let me go," she said, squirming from his arms. Stepping back, she bumped into a figure.

When she looked up and saw who it was, her legs grew rubbery. "Oh!" she gasped.

Alex said something very low and rapid in Greek to his brother, who looked at him angrily before turning and walking away.

Angela faced Alex, the blood pounding in her ears. "I—I thought you were in Athens," she said stupidly.

"So I was, but obviously I have returned." The look he bestowed upon her sent pinpricks of fire through her body.

"Mother has told me what you did for Miki. I must

119

add my thanks. It appears that you have one or two redeeming qualities after all." He spoke with irony, but came closer and put his hands lightly on her shoulders.

Angela's lips parted involuntarily, and she desperately tried to hold herself steady.

"Thank you, my girl, for your quick thinking. I can never repay you," Alex murmured huskily, kissing her quickly on each cheek.

He released her so suddenly that he almost pushed her from him. There was a brooding look in his eyes. "What about August, then? Are you going to stay and care for my children—now that you have learned how, through trial and error—or must I worry about what sorts of mischief they may get into?"

She suddenly saw that he truly wanted her to remain. Her heart skipped a couple of beats. Did he care for her, just a little?

Remember Petra, you fool, a warning voice said within her. He's just been buying her trousseau in Athens. Don't confuse a father's gratitude with your own foolish fantasies!

"Angela," he asked huskily. "What do you say?"

"I—yes. Yes, I'll stay."

Overwhelmed by her feelings, Angela turned and fled.

In her room, flinging herself on her bed, she shut her eyes tightly and clenched her fists. It was done. She had committed herself, and she felt depressed and exhilarated by turns. She knew she was being the worst kind of fool, and that her reason had completely left her. Yet, the thought of being near Alex and the children for more than another month overcame all other considerations.

This, then, was love. This was what her relationship with Rory had lacked. Angela didn't know whether to be glad she could feel such love for a man or sorry that the object of her affections was so far beyond her reach.

Now she didn't hesitate to write the letter to Rory she had been so dreading. There was no kind way of telling him that she didn't wish to marry him, but Angela did it as affectionately as she could. She emphasized that her life in Springport was too confining. She wished to travel, to expand her horizons. As gently as possible she concluded by saying that her feeling for him would always be strongly affectionate, but sisterly. Several times she contrived to mention Nancy. The more she thought about it, the more she wondered if Nancy and Rory might not be meant for each other the way everyone had always assumed she and Rory were.

Angela reread the letter a dozen times. When she was satisfied, she copied it onto a fresh piece of paper and put it into an envelope.

In spite of the uncertainty of her future, Angela felt enormously relieved at having made this decision at last.

She was just about to get into bed when some mysterious impulse drew her to the window. She saw Alex walking in the garden just outside. He was bare-chested, and seemed deep in thought.

Angela observed the moonlight glinting on his thick dark hair, creating a golden halo effect. More than ever he looked like her Apollo.

Alex paced restlessly, plucking a blossom of jasmine and putting it to his nostrils. He looked suddenly in her direction.

Hastily Angela drew back from the window. Could he have seen her watching him? Surely the curtains concealed her, and she had turned off her light.

When she had the courage to steal another look, she

noted that he had been joined by Niko, speaking in low, gruff tones in Greek.

Angela thought she caught Niko's question "What are you doing here?" but she couldn't understand Alex's reply.

The two men continued to converse. Niko became agitated and waved his arms. Although they kept their voices low, the tones became angry. Angela heard her name, then mention of Savvas, then Petra, and several times Caterina.

Niko seemed to be exhorting Alex. How Angela wished she could follow the conversation, instead of catching only one word in ten.

Finally they moved away. Watching Alex go, Angela felt as if he had taken a piece of her heart with him.

In the morning Stephanie came to fetch her. "Mother has been asking for you." Stephanie greeted Angela with a kiss. "She is giving me a cooking lesson and wants you, too."

Angela was delighted and followed Stephanie to the kitchen, where Mrs. Pallas smiled at her and spoke to her with gestures.

"Mother says you must watch and learn. All women should know how to cook, even if they don't need to do it. It is a question of feminine pride. Today we're doing moussaka."

"Great. That's my favorite. I'd love to know how to make it," Angela said. Cooking interested her, although she hadn't been particularly adventurous up to now.

She helped cut large eggplants and potatoes into slices. A filling of ground meat, herbs, spices, and tomato was already simmering on the stove.

Mrs. Pallas supervised as Angela helped Stephanie

layer the eggplant, potato, and filling. Then they made a béchamel sauce to put over the top, and set the dish in the oven to bake.

"Mother has been asking me questions about you, especially about your engagement. I was evasive, of course." Stephanie glanced reflectively at her.

Angela hesitated to say outright that she'd broken her engagement. "All I can say at the moment is that I've agreed to stay through August so that I can teach Miki and Crista English."

After Stephanie hugged her and related the good news to her mother, Mrs. Pallas cast Angela a shrewd look and smiled happily. "I understand," she murmured.

The family ate the moussaka at lunch, full of praises. Only Petra looked disdainful, while Alex appeared tired and somewhat gaunt. He was irritable and unsmiling, and began a stiff conversation with Angela about teaching materials for the children.

Even when Alex was speaking impersonally to her, the very sound of his thrilling voice, and the glitter in his intense eyes disoriented her. She had to dig her fingernails into her palms under the table to control her tremors.

It was apparent to her that Alex hadn't slept well and that something was upsetting him. His brow was furrowed with tension.

Fleetingly, Angela thought of how much she would like to put a cooling hand on his forehead, and immediately she felt her face redden under her tan.

Meanwhile Petra was speaking so loudly and dramatically to Niko that it was difficult not to listen to her conversation. It was in English, which convinced Angela that it was all for her benefit.

"Oh, yes, Alex bought a beautiful dress for me in this wonderful boutique in Athens, where I shall get

123

many of my clothes in future. In fact, Pavlos, the designer, has asked me to work up some designs for him and model them myself. . . ."

Alex, frowning, leaned closer to Angela. He wanted her to give his children a formal lesson every day for one hour in the morning, one in the afternoon. That was too much, Angela thought, but did not argue.

After lunch, when Angela went to change into her swimsuit, her room didn't look quite right. She couldn't at first put her finger on what was wrong. Then she noticed her wastebasket. It seemed to Angela that someone had gone through it. She remembered having crumpled the first draft of her letter to Rory into a ball and tossing it on top. But it was no longer there. Someone had removed the letter. Who? Why?

Angela grew warm and then angry that her privacy had been violated in this way. She should have been more careful, but still, she blushed at the thought of someone in the household reading that latter.

Stephanie was anything but sneaky and Alex was hardly the sort of person to go through someone's wastepaper basket. Savvas might, as a lark, but then he'd blurt out his indiscretion soon enough and make a joke of it. Niko was a possibility. He might wish to use such a letter to bolster his contention that Angela was after Savvas Pallas and the family fortune. It could, of course, have been Petra. Surely nobody was more underhanded than she.

Angela sighed and vowed to forget the incident. Whoever had taken the letter had already learned what he—or she—wished to know.

At the beach, Angela plunged into the cool water and swam effortlessly for quite some distance, keeping parallel with the island. She glided smoothly through the water with little noise or splashing. Then she turned and retraced her path, doing a backstroke. Suddenly she heard a commotion nearby. "Help," a female voice cried. *"Voithia,* help!"

It sounded like Petra, but Angela was too far away to make the figure out. It could have been Stephanie.

Rolling over on her stomach, Angela swam rapidly to the person in distress.

"Help! Alex!"

It *was* Petra. She was making a lot of noise and splashing as she treaded water, but she wasn't the least bit in trouble.

Silently Angela swam to Petra's side. She could see Alex already doing a swift stroke toward them. "If you insist on drowning," she told Petra calmly, "I'm afraid I'll have to save you, since I happen to be here on the spot, and Alex is still yards away."

Shooting Angela a look of the sheerest hatred, Petra whirled andswarm toward Alex. "It's nothing, *agápi mu,* I had a momentary cramp," she called out to him.

Angela, to avoid meeting Alex just then, silently dived beneath the water and swam until she could surface some distance from the couple. She climbed onto a rock, concealing herself from view, and pondered Petra's extraordinary behavior. Was her engagement, then, not as secure as everyone seemed to believe? Why else would she employ such a ruse, presumably to gain Alex's attention? Was he not attentive enough?

By the time Angela returned to the beach, Petra and Alex had gone. Only Savvas was there, playing with a deck of cards.

He smiled engagingly at Angela. "I was hoping you'd turn up. Come, sit here with me, and I'll tell your fortune."

With a practiced hand he shuffled cards and dealt them, casting her a mischievous look. "I learned everything from a gypsy girl in Paris. Many fortunes have

I told. They are always absolutely accurate, as you will see."

As he dealt out the cards he began to frown. "It can't be."

"What's the matter?"

"It can't be right."

"Am I to meet a handsome stranger?" she teased him.

"The cards say a tall man in your life. I'm not that tall," he grumbled. "It must be the lawyer across the sea."

Angela caught her breath slightly, a picture of Alex flashing in front of her. Not, of course, that she believed in fortune-telling.

"There's something to do with the numbers five and six. Both of them appear every time I deal the cards, but I don't know what they mean."

Angela thought for a moment. "Those are the ages of Miki and Crista."

"Of course. You're brilliant. I always said so. And look, there's something else. I keep getting the letters *DEL*. I wonder if it's short for the Delphic Oracle."

She smiled and shrugged.

"Oh, I've got it, Angelamou. It stands for Delos. We're taking a trip tomorrow, now that the *Crysula* has been repainted. We're going to Mykonos and Delos. You see? The cards never lie."

Angela smiled happily. "Oh, it will be exciting to see the sacred island of Delos for myself."

"Let me mix the cards again. Here and here and here." He made a few deft alterations. "Now listen to this. You have thought you were in love with one man, but it turns out you are madly in love with someone else. Who, you wonder? Why, a wonderful Greek who already loves you—wait, Angela!"

Savvas hastily scrambled to his feet and ran after

her. "What's the matter? Why do you run off like this? You know I have loved you from the minute I first saw you on the plane in Paris. I am serious, believe me. If only I had some money of my own! But Alex has put everything in trust for me until I get my degree, the devil take him. Even so, Angela, you will wait for me, please!"

He caught up to her and took her by the shoulders, brushing her cheek with his soft, quick kisses.

Angela felt her face burning. "It's impossible, Savvas. Aside from other considerations, I'm not Greek, I have no dowry, your family would never—"

"That is nothing, and the family already loves you. You have been a sister to Stephanie. And since saving Miki's life, don't you realize, Angelamou, that you are ours forever? Oh, curse my stupidity in not having finished my education. Alex has the real power now. And Mother and he are as close together as a cat and its whiskers."

Savvas suddenly frowned and looked guardedly at Angela, who had moved out of his reach and was walking slowly, keeping a space between them. She caught a shadow passing over his face. "What is it?" she asked.

"I will never lie to you, Angelamou. Although my family loves you, there *is* some objection to the two of us. I don't know what. But—but when I once or twice mentioned you to Alex, he nearly bit my head off. And Mother, who notices everything, told me to stop flirting with you because it was out of the question."

Angela felt a sinking in the pit of her stomach. So they disapproved of her as a marriage prospect for their son! Although she herself had suggested that this would be so, such confirmation made her feel wretched. Even if there had been no Petra, Alex would not have considered her!

127

Savvas, like the happy child he was, couldn't mope for long. "But just wait, Angelamou, until I win honors at university and come back to Greece to put Pallas Enterprises on a còmputer basis. Even the books will be written by computer, and illustrated, too."

"Do you think Stephanie will approve of that?" Angela teased him gently.

"By then my sister will have a child in each arm. She won't have room for a paintbrush."

Angela laughed, relieved that the conversation was restored to its usual levity, although underneath everything she had an aching heart that nothing could soothe.

"I'm going for a swim," Angela said, taking a running dive into the water.

"Wait for me. I haven't finished my proposal to you. First, we'll have a big party to celebrate. Then we'll be married in the biggest church in Athens, or else the smallest one on Mykonos. Whichever you want. Angela, wait!"

Chapter Nine

The next morning they set sail for Delos. In spite of the children's entreaties to be allowed to come, their father was firm in leaving them at home.

"The thing that bothers me," Stephanie whispered as she and Angela lay in the stern of the boat, sunbathing, "is that Petra stayed home as well. Imagine her remaining with my parents and the children when she could have been with Alex. She said she had a headache, but I don't believe it for a minute. Snakes don't get headaches. I think she's plotting something, and I don't like it."

Angela, remembering her missing letter, was inclined to agree that Petra might be up to something.

When they arrived at Delos, Savvas took Angela by the arm in a proprietary manner.

"Delos is supposed to have risen out of the sea, a gift from Poseidon to the nymph Leta, who was about to give birth to Apollo and Artemis," he related. "When the gods were born, the island magically blossomed with trees and flowers, and swans appeared. Nobody else was allowed to be born or to die here, and nobody lives here to this day—"

"Savvas, let Angela see for herself without blathering on like a tourist guide," Alex said in his low voice from behind them.

"What's biting you, Brother? I'm just giving her some background—"

"Surely she's read all about it already, haven't you, Angela?"

Although Alex was correct, Angela replied only with a nervous smile. She didn't wish to be the cause of contention between the brothers.

Alex studied her face with his probing eyes. "I, myself, like to experience something new in my own way, privately, absorbing every sensation, every nuance. Later I can fill in the details. I don't like bad movie music, Savvas, which you are providing. The kind that previews what the audience ought to be feeling, as well as telling what comes next—"

"Meanwhile, Brother, you haven't shut up yourself so that Angela could do what you just criticized me for not letting her do—"

"Shut up, everybody," said Stephanie, laughing. "We're coming to the sanctuary containing the Temple of Apollo."

Angela was disappointed to see a large square with only rudimentary stone remains.

"This is the base of the huge statue of Apollo that used to stand here," Savvas said, defying his brother. "A piece of the body is near the Temple of Artemis, and one foot of it is in the British Museum, a hand in the—"

"Oh, for God's sake!" Alex exploded. "You're not describing a murder and dismemberment, after all. We don't care where the various limbs have got to. Let's concentrate on what we can see right here."

Angela fervently wished the statue had been intact; she consoled herself by throwing surreptitious glances at her living Apollo. Striding through the ruins in white trousers and a white shirt, Alex looked very much at home in the birthplace of the god he so much resembled.

"Once the statue of Apollo had a giant bronze palm tree overlooking it," Stephanie said. "Just think—the temple painted every color of the rainbow, and inside, the most wonderful treasure of gold."

"Yes, I can imagine it," Angela said softly. There was an aura of opulence still, and she could picture the temple in its former splendor.

"Over there is the ancient agora, the marketplace," Niko said from behind Stephanie. "I'm sure Angela will be interested in seeing where things used to be bought and sold."

Angela knew that his remark had been aimed at her, and that it referred to his impression that she was a fortune hunter. Neither Stephanie nor Savvas reacted. What Alex might be thinking Angela couldn't say because he had concealed his eyes behind dark glasses.

They walked on across the Sacred Lake, now dry and dusty, and Angela gasped at the famous lions that seemed to be roaring into the pale blue sky. "Oh, how lovely they are," she exclaimed, while Stephanie beamed as if she herself had sculpted the long, lean-bodied creatures out of marble.

Throughout their wanderings on Delos Niko walked with Stephanie, and Angela found herself between Savvas and Alex. It was the first time that Petra had not been with the party and occupied all of Alex's attention. Now Angela noticed a strong tension between the brothers, which made her apprehensive. Savvas, although predictably attentive and somewhat flirtatious, made her uncomfortable, whereas Alex alternated between polite conversation and almost savage mockery.

Still, she found Alex's presence so electrifying that

he eclipsed Savvas's boyish prancing. It was Alex who made her go hot and cold by turns, who caused her uneven breathing and a weakness in her knees whenever his arm accidentally brushed against hers.

Later, while they sat at a café, Alex explained the history and archaeology of the island, deliberately concentrating on aspects that Angela would not have learned from a casual guide. She could have listened to his low, slightly husky voice indefinitely as he discussed the defeat of the Persians in the fifth century B.C. and continued past Hellenistic times and up through the Venetian and Turkish occupations. His narrative was most compelling, taking in aspects of the political and economic, as well as social conditions of each epoch. Savvas, though he had little tidbits of information, touched on things with a feather, whereas Alex probed with a scalpel.

"Let's have lunch at Mykonos," suggested Niko in a disgruntled tone. "Nothing here but a tourist pavilion and 'le sandwich'!"

Angela was absolutely enchanted by the dazzling white town of Mykonos. The houses resembled the ones on the Pallas island, with rounded corners and thick white surfaces that looked like sugary icing dripping down a cake.

She admired the marvelous windmills, lovely, graceful structures with thatch tops, like straw hats, and funny triangular bits of sails attached to the creaking frames driven by the wind.

"I'll take you to see the churches, Angela," Savvas promised, winking at her. "Some people say there is one church for every day of the year."

The five browsed in the boutiques selling ethnic clothes as well as jewelry, Byzantine icons, brass scales, and handwoven rugs. Angela bought a pair of sandals and a lovely embroidered white skirt and matching blouse, refusing to let Savvas pay for them.

Niko took the opportunity to hiss at her. "Easy to refuse a small gift when you are looking forward to a lifetime of riches."

Angela paled and moved out of Niko's path. Whenever she was feeling relaxed, he managed to say something to spoil her good mood.

They ate facing the water, where they could watch the boats and the procession of chic tourists who were promenading up and down the main drag.

"*Ciao*, Alex!" A group of very attractive young men and girls passed by. Alex jumped up to greet them, and spoke to them in rapid Italian.

"Those are friends of Alex's from Milan," Stephanie told Angela. "We'll see them later at the disco."

Angela hated herself for the pang of jealousy that went through her when she noticed Alex smiling at a richly dressed, statuesque redhead.

"He—he speaks Italian so fluently," she whispered.

"Of course," Stephanie replied. "Alex speaks about seven languages. Didn't you know?"

Angela was saved from answering by Savvas. "Try some of these *kalamarákia,* fried baby squid. They're beautiful, just like you."

After lunch they took a taxi to one of the loveliest beaches on the island, a long expanse of white sand, virtually deserted. As Stephanie and Angela started to walk along the water's edge, Savvas doggedly followed them.

"Not now, Savvas. I hardly ever get a moment alone with Angela. I want to discuss my wedding. You'll be bored to tears."

"Who, me?" Savvas did a mock pirouette. "I will be best man."

"Oh, Savvas, you know that Niko has already chosen Alex as best man," Stephanie corrected him impatiently.

"All right, second best man, then. As long as I am first best with Angela. By the way, do you think Alex will make it a double wedding with Petra?" asked Savvas, kicking a flat rock along the wet sand near the shore.

Angela felt a gripping pain near her heart, and then a warmth suffused her that had nothing to do with the sun.

"Not on your life," said Stephanie fiercely. "If Alex must marry that snake, he won't do it at my wedding!"

"Ah, well," said Savvas mildly, "Papa always wanted Pallas books to be printed on Leonidas paper. You can't really blame Alex—"

"Certainly I blame Alex! If you're so concerned with the family welfare all of a sudden, why don't you marry Petra yourself? Alex declined the privilege once before."

"My dear sister, there are many things I would do for the family fortune, but marrying is not one of them. When I marry, it will be little Angela here, I swear it." Savvas spoke so emphatically that Stephanie stopped short and looked at her brother sharply. She shifted her gaze to Angela.

Angela shook her head and smiled wanly. "It is only a game that he plays."

"No game, I assure you," Savvas said. "Just wait. I have ways of insinuating myself, of making myself lovable. Such as weaving you a crown of jasmine every day, and bringing you wonderful things to eat and drink, and telling you of your beauty in a thousand different ways—"

Angela could stand no more. She ran to the water

and dived in, feeling the welcome coolness of the waves wash over her and soothe her turbulent feelings.

Savvas raced after Angela, leaving Stephanie standing on the beach, shaking her head with exasperation.

Savvas, like all the family, swam like a fish. He easily caught Angela, playfully pretending to be a whale, a walrus, and finally a shark, giving her little nips on her arms and shoulders.

They waited for Stephanie, and then all three returned to the spot where they had left Niko and Alex. They found two sullen men who appeared not to be on speaking terms, nor would either tell the others the reason.

Stephanie snuggled up to Niko and tried to put him in a better humor, but he only grunted and scowled, burying his face in a blanket.

Without a word Alex jumped up, tore off his sunglasses, and took a running dive into the sea. He went through the surf like a propeller, but silently, barely turning his head to breathe or lifting his powerful arms out of the water. Angela imagined how wonderful it would be to swim with him, with no necessity for speech—

"Don't you ever listen to a word I say?" Savvas cried petulantly, breaking into her fanciful dream.

"I'm sorry, Savvas. What was it?"

"Are you staying on in August?"

"Uh, yes, I am. I'm going to be teaching the children English—"

"Pah, you just want to be near me, and that's the truth, Angelamou. Your lawyer across the sea has faded from memory."

"Savvas, leave Angela alone and don't meddle in something you don't understand," Stephanie sharply admonished.

135

Angela lay down, surrendering her face to the sun, and shut her eyes. A rainbow of colors flashed in front of her eyelids, and in a little while she was asleep.

That evening they went to a café-bar that attracted a chic international clientele. A guitarist was playing softly and singing romantic songs in French.

Niko and Alex had made up after their quarrel to the extent that they were icily polite to each other, without their easy cameraderie. Stephanie had confided to Angela that Niko wouldn't tell her what was wrong between them.

Angela had a nagging feeling that the quarrel had something to do with her. Was Niko trying to convince Alex that she had designs on his brother? Certainly both Niko and Alex stared at her gloomily when she appeared wearing the outfit she had purchased that afternoon. Only Stephanie and Savvas complimented on the success of her dress, and noted how Greek she looked. Angela felt ill at ease. Did Alex and Niko think she was pretending to go native? In fact, she had simply liked the thin white material, the classic lines, and the fine white embroidery. Anyway, several of the well-turned-out Italian girls were wearing Greek clothes, but nobody had directed such dark looks toward them.

Several times Angela had the fleeting thought that she should try to speak to Niko, but she kept hesitating, fearing she might reveal her feelings about Alex. How Niko would rage to learn that she did not covet the younger, unattached brother but the very one who was engaged, and who controlled the family fortune to boot.

The songs sung by the guitarist were making Angela very sad. Of all the men to have fallen in love with,

Alex Pallas surely was the worst possible choice. From the corner of her eye Angela was aware of him sitting tensely at the table, drumming his fingers nervously on it. He still wore his sunglasses. Something surely was bothering him. Suddenly Alex jumped to his feet, turning over his drink in the abruptness of his motion. "I've had enough of these maudlin songs. Let's go to the discotheque. Do you mind, Angela?" he asked.

Every time Alex said her name, a ripple of flame went through her. Would he dance with her? And if he asked her, could she trust herself to accept?

Alex's friends were already seated when the Pallas party entered the huge, noisy place, and he was immediately swallowed up by the Italians.

Angela, who couldn't say more than hello and goodbye in Italian, felt dejected and left out, until Alex abruptly turned to her. "I hope you aren't bored, Angela. I know we're being rather rude, but we haven't seen each other in ages."

"No, of course not. It's all right," Angela said, trying to look as if she meant it.

"You don't speak Italian?" he asked.

She shook her head, murmuring that she had studied Spanish. Alex clicked his tongue and asked about the American education system, which did not encourage more than one foreign language. "You could easily pick up some French and Italian," he told her. "Judging from how quickly you're learning Greek, you have a facility."

Because of the noise, Angela had to lean a little closer to Alex to hear. He had deserted the Italians in her favor after all, and little by little she found herself telling him about college, Stephanie, her sister and her Aunt Emily. Alex was so attentive, so responsive, that she lost her nervousness. He was sitting very close to her, filling her glass with wine. She felt an intimacy she had never known with him before.

"You sound as if you have enjoyed your life very much," he remarked, his eyes probing hers.

"I—I have, up to now. But—but I have always wished to break away from the smallness of my world. I feel so—so provincial here in Europe, where I keep meeting multilingual people, well-traveled." Angela stopped and bit her lip. She was making a fool of herself. What could Alex possibly care that she had never traveled? Even worse, wasn't she practically hinting for an invitation. . . ?

Whatever Alex might have thought of her remarks she would never learn. Greek music was now being played, and everyone's attention turned to the small knots of Greek men who got up to dance.

Angela was fascinated, at the same time thinking wryly that only in such a male-dominated society could men dare to dance with each other without looking foolish. Indeed, it was a most masculine impression they gave, dancing side by side, their measured, authoritative steps quite exciting to watch.

"Ópa, ópa," the crowd was yelling.

"There goes Savvas," Stephanie shouted to Angela.

Sure enough, Savvas had leaped to the center of the floor, snapping his fingers and bending and jumping with the others.

Their table was at the edge of the dance floor. When Savvas smiled at Angela, she returned it and was noticed by Niko. He snorted contemptuously. "You think that is dancing, eh? Savvas has spent too much time in Paris. I will show you what dancing is. Come, Alex."

Alex frowned and shook his head. "No, really, I'm not in the mood—"

"Come on, come on, it will change your mood. We must show up these terrible amateurs. Besides—" Here he switched to Greek.

Perhaps it was a challenge. Alex stood up, his expression stubborn, as if he had accepted a dare. Taking a last gulp of wine, Alex went out on the floor with Niko, who had produced a handkerchief. He held one end aloft, and Alex took the other.

Stephanie moved next to Angela. "Alex hasn't danced in years, not since Caterina died. Oh, look, Ange, look at my Niko!"

Angela could do nothing *but* look with rapt attention. When Savvas spied the the other two, he moved over to them. The three did a wonderful dance together, twirling, stomping, and leaping into the air. They were by far the best dancers on the floor.

To Angela's mind, Savvas was nimble, Niko flamboyant, but Alex was the most graceful, the most masculine, the most compelling. When Alex knelt, or leaped, or raised his arms in the air and snapped his fingers, he seemed to be doing a dance of seduction, almost, for his beloved. His face had a look of passionate intensity that thrilled her. How high he held his head, tossing his hair back from his eyes. How powerful he was. And then he looked at her, and she felt she would swoon with longing—until a moment later she noticed that Carla, the attractive Italian redhead, was seated only slightly behind her. Had Alex been looking at her, at Carla, or at them both? Oh, how Angela wished that Alex were doing that dance for her, and her alone.

When Niko later asked Angela to dance, she said yes with the greatest of hesitation, fearing he would take this opportunity to be nasty to her. However, the rock music was deafening, and if Niko had any such intention, he abandoned it. He did, however, fix her with his hard, hooded stare that she found so disconcerting.

Before she could sit down, Savvas claimed her for his partner, and Stephanie danced with Niko. As for Alex, he took Carla onto the floor and smiled at her steadily.

Strange feelings of jealousy assailed Angela. She was behaving like a silly adolescent having her first crush on a boy. Still, she felt as she felt. Maybe she had fallen so hard for Alex because he was her first love. Certainly Rory had never caused the slightest turmoil within her.

Savvas kept Angela on the floor for several dances. When Angela was able to search out Alex with her eyes she found him seated at the table again. His companions were talking and laughing, but he was sitting silently, brooding, looking miserable.

"Those Italians are jet-setters," Savvas shouted to Angela. "Sailing in Greece, gambling on the Riviera, canoeing in South America, skiing in Gstaad, attending film festivals in Cannes and Taormina. Alex used to spend a lot of time with them, when he wasn't working his head off. Last summer we thought something would develop between him and Carla, but nothing did."

Angela asked shakily, "Does Alex—care for this Carla, do you think? But feels he has to marry Petra—"

"Pah, who knows? He's deeper than the Mediterranean, that one. I can assure you, he doesn't confide in me. In Niko, maybe. To Alex I'm the baby brother, the pest."

After the number, Angela begged to be released but Savvas took her arm tightly. "Please, this one is slow."

Gathering her close to him, Savvas held her dreamily, nipping at her earlobe gently with his soft lips.

Angela was almost in a trance from the wine as

well as the rhythm of the music, and she followed Savvas's lead, hardly aware of what her feet were doing.

Abruptly Savvas stopped dancing. Glancing behind him, Angela saw Alex looming, his mouth tight and angry.

"That's enough! You don't only dance, you make a public display!" He continued in Greek, and his words drew a sullen shake of the head from Savvas, who was, in the end, defeated by his older brother's force of personality. Savvas went back to the table.

Just as Angela started to follow Savvas, she felt Alex's hand on her arm. It was like an electric current passing through her body.

"You won't dance with me?" he asked her huskily.

"Yes, of course," she murmured, feeling her cheeks color.

Alex put his arm around her waist, taking her hand in his. Her fingers felt like icicles being melted by a flame.

The top of her head came to his shoulder so she couldn't see his face, but she felt the exquisite pressure he applied to her back through the thin material of her blouse. It was as if she were being branded with a hot iron. Alex held her firmly, but not too near to him. He danced very smoothly. Angela followed him blindly, feeling stiff and frightened.

Suddenly several rather boisterous dancers came onto the floor, pushing Angela violently from behind. She was crushed against Alex, and it became so crowded that they couldn't break apart. For a few breathless minutes they stood pressed together, scarcely moving their feet, while Angela couldn't tell if she felt the thumping of her heart alone or if it was mingled with the beating of his. The hard length of his body, from his chest to his thighs, squeezed tightly against her, thrilling her beyond endurance.

141

They remained like that until the music stopped. The next number was in a fast tempo, and as if by magic the crowd dispersed. For one moment more Alex held her close to him, increasing the pressure of his hands on her back. She didn't move a muscle, afraid even to breathe. Then he released her. Their eyes locked, and both immediately looked elsewhere. Holding her elbow, he led her back to the table. Frantically Angela bit her lips and dug her nails into the palms of her hands, trying to control her trembling.

I love him, she thought, over and over. Oh, God, I love him terribly. What am I going to do!

There was nothing she could do but take a seat at the table. Now the Italians drew Angela into their circle, pouring wine into her glass and paying her a great deal of attention. They spoke reasonable English, and Angela entered the conversation shyly at first, then more eagerly.

During a lull Angela looked for Alex and found him dancing with Carla. A jealous sigh escaped her involuntarily when she saw how closely Alex held his partner. Angela was nothing special to him. Suddenly she was miserable with longing and despair. It was too warm, and the smoke stung her eyes. While the others were deciding how much wine to order, Angela took the opportunity to slip out of the discotheque and onto the cool streets.

It was a welcome relief to breathe in the fresh night air and bask in the silence. Angela walked slowly through the charming twisting streets. Although there was no lighting, the startling white of the buildings and even the sidewalks created a ghostly brightness. She was fascinated by the network of the streets, some of them so narrow that a person could lean out of a window and touch the house across the way.

As Angela turned corner after corner she was enchanted to find a plane tree or mulberry putting crazily up from a tiny whitewashed cube. Wonderful pink oleander bushes and scarlet hibiscus plants were tucked into little squares, and possibly a trailing green pepper plant. From the open windows she heard strains of bouzouki music.

When she had cooled her burning cheeks, Angela turned and headed back. She wasn't quite sure of the way, but in the distance she could make out the choppy sea. Suddenly the wind began blowing strongly. The velocity increased by the moment, as gusts tousled her hair into golden swirls around her head and her skirt was whipped against her legs. The wind made a mournful sound that echoed along the narrow alleyways.

Angela felt uneasy. She was not sure of her bearings, and the howling added to her feeling of vulnerability.

When a hand reached out and grabbed her arm, Angela screamed in fright.

"Be quiet, you silly woman," demanded Niko in his harsh voice.

Angela nearly fainted with relief one moment, becoming quite agitated the next, because he was holding her arm in a steely grip. "Why are you wandering the streets? Who are you meeting?"

"Nobody," she murmured. "This is my first trip to Mykonos, as you know very well."

Niko snorted. "I don't know any such thing. I think you tell stories. Stephanie trusts you, of course, but you can't fool me so easily."

"Please, Niko, my—my arm."

He relaxed his grip. "Come, I'll take you back—"

"I can find my own way," she snapped, and immediately regretted it. Niko snorted again, suspicious that she had been meeting somebody.

"Why are you staying until the end of August?" he asked her, keeping a firm hold on her arm as he steered her down the street. "Why are you so interested in Alex's children? What kind of engagement do you have to that lawyer? If I'm wrong about you and Savvas, then what *are* you after?"

"I'm not after anything. Alex asked me to teach the children English and I accepted, that's all. I think Crista and Miki are darling, but then I'm a teacher and I like most children. I'm also enjoying being in Greece with Stephanie. We are best friends, and for four years at college she talked of almost nothing but Greece. If you can't understand any of this, there's no way I can explain it better. I just wish, Niko, that you'd stop jumping out of dark corners and frightening me."

"I think every word you say is a lie." Tightening his grip, Niko tried to embrace her.

A sudden fury took hold of Angela, giving her the strength to break loose. Racing blindly down the snaking streets, she had no idea where she was but knew only that she must head toward the sea.

When Angela finally reached the harbor, she was breathless, but still angry. This business with Niko would have to stop. She had no intention of returning to the discotheque now and looked instead for the *Crysula*. The wind had reached gale force, and Angela found it difficult to walk.

To her dismay, Alex was standing in front of the boat as if waiting for her. "You have ignored what I told you about going out by yourself at night. I don't like my wishes disobeyed!"

Although she couldn't see him very well, Angela heard his angry tone clearly. "I—I was feeling warm, and the smoke bothered my eyes. I just wanted a breath of air. I'm sorry." She wasn't really, but it seemed easier to apologize to Alex than to stand there arguing with him about her independence. Besides, if she had listened to him, she would have avoided the unpleasant encounter with Niko.

Her apology did not appease Alex. "We didn't know what had happened to you. Niko went out looking for you—"

"He found me," she murmured in a low voice.

"Did he? Where is he, then?"

"I—I'm tired, and I'd like to go to bed, if I may," she said dejectedly. She felt awkward, one hand trying to keep her skirt from blowing around her legs and the other brushing her hair from her eyes.

"Don't go yet, please, Angela," Alex requested, his voice suddenly soft.

She felt her blood turn to liquid fire. Before she could decide what to answer, she heard Niko's voice shouting angrily in Greek.

Alex shouted back at him, and the two advanced upon each other, fists clenched. Angela was terrified that they were going to have a fight, and yet she didn't dare get between them and implore them to stop it.

Just then Savvas appeared at the railing of the boat and yelled something to the other two.

"What?" shouted Alex. "Oh, my God!" Without appearing to notice what he was doing, he put his arm around Angela and drew her toward the rope ladder.

Niko had already vaulted aboard and was shouting instructions to Savvas.

"But what's the matter?" Angela kept asking. The wind had grown so loud that her voice couldn't be heard above the tumult.

It was obvious that they were setting sail, although they were supposed to have remained overnight in Mykonos. The men were busy casting off, so Angela went below in search of Stephanie. She found her

145

friend, white-faced and nervous, pacing in her cabin. "Mother just phoned to say that the children have run away."

"Oh, no! Is she sure? I mean, they aren't playing a game—"

Stephanie shook her head vigorously. "They left a note. Miki can write a bit. It said they were taking their kitten away. It makes no sense. They don't even have a kitten. One thing I can tell you: Petra is behind it. I knew she was cooking up a plot, the evil witch. If anything happens to the children, I'll murder her myself!"

Angela compressed her lips, certain that Stephanie was correct about Petra's involvement in the affair.

The boat began to rock alarmingly. It was going to be a very rough journey. Stephanie, putting her hand to her head, suddenly fell across her bunk. "I don't feel well. It was all the drinking, I think. Go up on deck, Ange. It's better up there."

Since there was little Angela could do to help Stephanie, she fought her way up on deck, where she nóticed Savvas standing against the rail, his head over the side.

Niko flung up his arms in contempt, shouting to Alex, "Some sailor! Two waves and he's had it. What are you doing here?" he continued, turning his anger on Angela.

"I—I can help, if you need another pair of hands—"

Niko cast skeptical eyes at the sky, but Alex came forward. "Are you all right, Angela?"

"Yes. I have sailed before. If there's anything I can do—"

Alex nodded and began to give instructions. Niko, unfortunately, didn't know the sailing terminology in English. Jib, mainsail, winch, meant nothing to him, and things had to be said twice, which infuriated him.

Alex remained remarkably patient, in spite of being obviously worried sick over his children.

Keeping a cool head, Angela followed Alex's directions to the letter. She, too, was anxious about Crista and Miki and was impatient for them to reach the island as quickly as possible. The vicious wind, although whipping the sails and sending great, chopping waves crashing onto the deck, aided them to get back in record time.

The three were soaked through. Alex ripped off his shirt and flung off his shoes. He dived into the churning surf and swam for shore, while Niko and Angela anchored the boat and furled the sails. By the time Niko had lowered the dinghy into the water, Alex was running up the beach.

At the house Angela found a terrible commotion. Every light was on, and she could see the hurricane lamps of the island workers dotting the darkness. Everyone was out searching for the children.

Stephanie and Savvas, still pale and uncomfortable, nevertheless went with Angela to the living room. There stood Petra, being confronted by Maria. The maid, crying and sobbing, was pointing an accusing finger at Petra. From Stephanie, her eyes blazing as she translated, Angela gathered that Maria was claiming that Petra had threatened to drown the children's kitten, and they had fled with it.

Petra curled her lip disdainfully and denied the whole story. She maintained that the children were simply teasing, as usual. Furthermore, when Petra glimpsed Angela standing in the doorway, she added that Angela herself had encouraged the children to be disobedient to her.

"That's a lie and you know it," shouted Stephanie.

Mr. Pallas looked uncomfortably from one to the other, not knowing quite what to believe. Mrs. Pallas,

147

pale and upset, was staring at Petra with her lips pursed, although she said nothing.

Alex rushed into the room with hurricane lamps. "That's enough bickering! First we'll find my children and then we'll get to the bottom of this business."

Chapter Ten

Angela took the hurricane lamp she was handed and started out with the others to search for the children. Stephanie and Niko were slightly ahead of her and apparently didn't realize she was so close to them. They were speaking English, as they often did together, to give Niko practice.

"I don't want to contradict you, my love," Stephanie was saying, "but I don't think you have any idea of how far Petra will go—"

"Nonsense. You're simply prejudiced in favor of your friend. Petra is the wronged one in all this and always has been. Engaged to Alex from childhood, she is first humiliated when he marries Caterina. But Petra forgives and forgets. Just as she will get Alex, finally, along comes this penniless American, leaving her boyfriend behind, making trouble, flirting with Savvas, trying to win the children away from Petra—"

"That's a lie," declared Stephanie. "The children have never liked Petra, and they loved Angela from the first minute, just as I did. Angela would never do anything to hurt anyone—"

"Wouldn't she! Remember, Stephanie, that you are Greek. Remember the ways of your people. Do you want Savvas to be made a fool of? You saw what happened when Alex married that nobody from nowhere, that terrible Caterina. Now Savvas goes around with lovesick eyes like a lamb enticed by a she-wolf—oh, a pretty one, I grant you—and Alex is even more upset. . . ."

Angela had to force herself to veer off the main path. Her face was hot and tears stung her eyes. She felt helpless to deal with Niko's distrust and hatred of her. Also, she felt guilty. Her love for Alex had nothing to do with his wealth, but Niko had correctly perceived that her heart was occupied in Greece, not America, and that her stubborn presence on the island made no sense unless she was concealing a secret love.

Impatiently Angela brushed at her wet lashes. This was not the time to think of her own troubles. Her first concern was the children.

Anxiously Angela shined her lamp back and forth. "Miki, Crista," she called, over and over. The only reply was the wind mournfully whistling through the trees. How cold the children must be, how miserable, Angela thought, as tears momentarily blinded her. Petra's cruelty was overwhelming. The children had been visiting Tutu in Petra's room, hoping she would relent and let them keep the kitten with them. Nobody else in the household—except Maria, who fed it—knew of its existence. Angela could well understand that if Petra had threatened to drown the kitten, the children would have fled with it. But where?

As Angela went groping through the harsh underbrush she blamed herself again and again for what had happened. After the first episode, it had been her duty to go to Alex and tell him everything she had learned from the children, regardless of whether or not he chose to believe her. She had known that Petra was a potential danger to Crista and Miki, and she should have informed him of that fact. Angela grew more sick with worry every moment. If any harm came to the children, it would be at least partly her fault.

She came to the end of the path. The rest was sheer rock and led up to an unscalable mountain. The children couldn't possibly be up there.

Dejected, Angela started back, still shining her lamp and calling the children's name every few minutes. She felt exhausted and chilled through, since she had never dried off from her spraying on the boat. Her feet were blistered and her bare legs were slashed by thistles.

When she finally came within sight of the house, she saw that all the rooms were still illuminated. On the hill behind the house lamps continued to move in the darkness. It was two-thirty in the morning. Crista and Miki had been missing for more than six hours, and Angela felt her panic rising. Where could they possibly have hidden? She couldn't bear to return to the house just then. Instead, she made for her private sanctuary, the olive grove. There it was as peaceful as always, although the wind still blew briskly.

Angela stood still suddenly, listening, not daring to breathe. Had she heard the mewing of a kitten, or was it only the wind? Straining her ears to catch another sound through the soft stirrings of the leaves in the olive trees, she flashed her lamp on the ground and then raised it into the air. A few feet away from her, on the lowest branch of an olive tree, she saw the glitter of cat's eyes, and next to them the huddled forms of the children.

"Miki, Crista," she called softly. "Wake up now, darlings. Don't be frightened," she said softly in Greek as two sleepy little faces stared down at her. "Give me Tutu. Don't worry, nobody will harm it."

Miki handed down the kitten, and Angela took it, tears of relief streaming down her cheeks and moistening the animal's soft fur.

"We couldn't get down," Crista sobbed. "We yelled and yelled. And then we fell asleep."

After they were safe at her feet, Angela knelt and embraced them briefly. "Let's go home now."

Crista was so sleepy that Angela had to carry her, while Miki walked at her side, holding the kitten. Both children were utterly exhausted, and Angela herself was ready to collapse. She had been walking for three hours.

All the searchers had gone far afield. If Angela hadn't found the children, they would have had to remain where they were until daylight, since the wind made it impossible for their cries to be heard more than a couple of feet away.

As they started up the front steps the door flew open and Stephanie rushed out. "Angela's found them! They're safe!"

In spite of her ordeal Angela awoke very early the next morning, too restless to remain in bed. Emerging from her room, she found that the entire household still slept, with the exception of the children. They were so happy to see her that they jumped on her with cries and kisses.

Over breakfast they told her their story. Petra had insisted that Angela was going away and that *she* would teach them English in the future. If they didn't obey her now, she would make them sorry when she became their mother. When they protested, she grew very angry and threatened to drown their kitten.

"Shh, shh, it's all over now," Angela said, trying to soothe them. At least the story of the kitten was out in the open, and they now had it in their own room.

"You won't go away, will you, Angela?" Miki asked anxiously.

"I don't want Petra to be our mother," Crista added, beginning to cry.

Angela comforted them the best she could, evading a direct answer to their questions. "Tell your father the whole story," Angela advised. "Don't be afraid. He won't punish you."

She realized that she couldn't say anything to Alex after all. She was too biased, too much involved, to give Alex a straight account of her rival's activities. Besides, if she tried to talk to him, he surely would realize—how she felt about him. Concealing her love was becoming more difficult every moment.

At lunch only Stephanie and Savvas joined the children and Angela. This time when the two questioned their niece and nephew, they received a complete explanation.

"Petra will leave the house today, I swear it!" Stephanie said between angry bites of her lunch. "We must tell Alex immediately. Pull him out of bed by his feet, if necessary."

Savvas stroked the air with the palm of his hand. "I've already tried. I've seen Alex. He won't listen to a word, and told me to mind my own business. Just imagine! And don't forget that your precious Niko also sticks up for Petra."

"Yes, we'll see about that," Stephanie said grimly, pushing back her chair.

Angela sighed with dejection. It was no use. Alex must love Petra very much to ignore what was so plain in front of his nose.

Savvas proposed giving Angela a Greek lesson at the beach. "I have brought you a grammar. That is the hardest part of learning this language."

It certainly was. Surprisingly, for a fellow with a short attention span, Savvas was a good teacher. Angela concentrated very hard, grateful to take her mind from other matters. Although she could follow simple sentences and her vocabulary was increasing, she needed to learn the structure of the language.

While she worked, Savvas encouraged her with compliments. "That's right, you must learn quickly so that when we are ready to marry, you will be able to converse fluently."

Angela raised her eyes from her book. "For the last time, will you drop it, please, Savvas."

"What's the matter? I thought you were beginning to like me."

"Of course I like you. Like a sister. But just now I'm confused about the possessives of neuter nouns. . . ."

After awhile, Savvas was called from the house by his mother. It had become extremely hot and close, and Angela decided on a swim. When she dived into the water, however, she realized how truly tired she was from lack of sleep, and she turned over on her back. As she floated she grew more relaxed. When her head bumped into an object, she twisted around, startled, and found that it was Niko. His dark curls were dripping and his face, close to hers, looked mean and angry. Without a word he grabbed her and forced his lips against hers.

She spluttered and twisted her head free. "Don't," she implored fearfully.

"You can pull the wool over some people's eyes, but not these eyes," Niko spat at her. "You little tramp—" He pushed her head into the water.

In a panic, Angela lashed out and hit him in the face. Making an enormous effort, she wiggled free of him and swam ashore, aware that he was close behind.

She came out of the water, breathless, and turned to face him furiously. "This must stop once and for all! Come with me to Stephanie. I'm going to tell her everything! I've only hesitated because I didn't want to hurt her, but I think it will hurt her far more to marry someone like you. She's the dearest, most trusting girl in the world and doesn't deserve someone who sneaks around behind her back the way you've been doing, treating me like dirt—"

"Exactly. Treating you as you deserve! And I'm not the only one sneaking around," Niko shouted, his eyes burning like charcoal.

"I don't know what you're talking about," she shouted back.

He snorted and shook the water off him, like a shaggy dog.

Angela hastily pulled her sundress over her wet bikini. "I'd like to know what proof you have against me. Your hostility is bad enough, but those disgusting insinuations, and—and the way you grab me, as if I were—as if I were—" Angela trailed off, flustered.

"And aren't you?" Niko asked insolently.

For some moments they regarded each other angrily. Niko touched his face, which was still red from the blow she'd given him.

"I'm sorry for hitting you," she whispered, appalled at her uncharacteristic behavior. "But, really, you frightened the wits out of me. I thought you meant to hold my head under the water—"

"Don't be silly. I was just trying to scare the truth out of you, for once. All I've heard so far are lies. Oh, Stephanie believes you. She wouldn't recognize the devil himself if he appeared in horns and tail. She is too trusting, but I know better. I saw you before, with Savvas, with your heads together—"

"For goodness' sake, he's teaching me Greek, that's all."

"Oh, I see. You're learning Greek. Imagine that." Niko smirked at her scornfully. "I can see why you want to learn Greek! After all, it is spoken in every country of the world, isn't it! You sneaky little liar. You don't fool me for a minute. You expect me to believe that you would leave your boyfriend and stay here to teach a couple of kids you never saw before? And you yourself are learning Greek! I'll tell you what I believe."

Niko put his scowling face closer to hers. "I believe in your greed, your itch to get your fingers into the Pallas fortune. More than that, I think the boyfriend is in on the whole thing. It's easy enough for a beautiful girl to get a stupid nincompoop like Savvas to marry her. Then you divorce, get a handsome settlement, the boyfriend appears as number-two husband, with a fortune between his fingers—"

"For God's sake, where did you get that incredible nonsense? It sounds like a bad American movie. Tell me, Niko, did you actually ever meet an American before?"

"Don't be smart with me and change the subject. You know what I'm talking about. First you tried to make trouble between Petra and Alex—"

"I did no such thing," Angela broke in hotly, her face reddening nevertheless. "I've never even mentioned her to Alex—"

"Of course not. You fixed it with the children, who can't see through you like I can, and with Stephanie. She was waiting outside my door this afternoon to give me an argument! My own sweet Stephanie, who, before you put ideas into her head, wouldn't ever have questioned my judgment."

"I said nothing! The children told her, and she can see with her own eyes—"

"She sees what you want her to see! You were always the clever one, she admits that. You have made trouble

156

between us and between Alex and me. Savvas, that idiot, deserves you—except that if you got your hooks into him, the whole Pallas family would suffer. It's enough that Alex made a stupid marriage. I don't want to see it happen again."

"In that case," Angela retorted in a quavering voice, "take a good look at the way the children react to Petra. Ask them, if you dare. It has nothing to do with me. . . ."

Niko's eyes narrowed. Muttering in Greek, he grabbed her wrists in his hard hands. "Look at me and tell me you don't want to marry Savvas."

"Of course I don't want to marry Savvas," Angela shouted at him in exasperation. All her New England reserve had deserted her in the face of Niko's attack. "I'm fond of him in a sisterly way, that's all!"

"Then tell me the real reason you are staying for an extra month. Quickly, now, no more lies. I knew the moment I saw you that it was going to be a summer-long business. In fact, I had a bet with Alex that it was so, and I've won." Niko's tone was smug and hateful.

"It was Alex himself who asked me to stay! He wouldn't have let me teach the children for only one month—"

"Pah! That big Tarzan of yours in America is waiting for you to come home. There he sits, the boyfriend, sweating in his hot little office, waiting, and waiting—"

"Stop it," Angela said suddenly, as tears filled her eyes. "He isn't waiting anymore. I've broken the engagement."

"Aha!" Niko was triumphant. He dropped her hands as if they were a pair of poisonous scorpions.

"Anyway, you knew that," Angela accused Niko.

"Of course I didn't. How could I?"

"You saw the letter," she went on. "It must have been you. Someone took the first draft of my letter to Rory right out of my wastepaper basket."

Niko didn't deny it. He merely looked at her thoughtfully, suddenly grown calm. "So you broke your engagement, and you want me to believe it had nothing to do with Savvas. And you didn't tell Stephanie."

"Yes. I mean, I haven't told her yet." Angela flushed deeply. "I realized I'd—I'd made a mistake. You're right about one thing, I guess. If I'd really—really loved Rory, I wouldn't have wanted to stay in Greece for so long. That's why I wrote to call it off. But it has nothing whatever to do with Savvas." She paused for breath, wondering why she was confiding all this to her declared enemy.

"And that is your only reason." Niko snorted derisively. "You made a mistake. It has nothing to do with the Pallas riches."

"Nothing whatsoever," Angela said coolly, looking Niko in the eye. "There are rich men in Boston. I didn't have to come all the way to Greece to go after Savvas, especially when I'd never even met him before."

"I see. Then it's for love of the children that you stay here all summer."

"Why not? I do love them. They're very lovable."

He looked steadily at her. "What's so special about these children?"

"Surely you can see that for yourself. Besides, they're so—so vulnerable, and they haven't any mother—" Angela turned away to hide her tears. She, too, had lost her mother at an early age. She knew what it had meant to have her dear Aunt Emily. . . .

"You care more for Crista and Miki than Petra does?"

"Petra doesn't care for them at all," said Angela, sniffing. "She'd make them miserable. She has already begun. She threatened to drown their kitten. That was why they ran away. Ask them yourself, if you don't believe me." Angela fumbled in her beach bag for something to wipe her eyes.

"Do you think Petra would make Alex miserable?"

Angela blew her nose, but her fingers began to tremble.

"You think Alex is such a fool that he wouldn't be aware of all this, if it were true?" Niko persisted.

Angela kept her eyes down. She was on dangerous ground, and found herself saying too emphatically, "Of course Alex isn't a fool! I mean—perhaps he—he feels guilty over what happened in the past. His father wants the marriage so much, and—and Petra is beautiful, of course. . . ."

"Is it only the children you care for? Or is it also Alex?"

Unprepared for Niko's sly question, Angela gasped and shut her eyes, feeling the color flood into her face. She hesitated a second too long. "I—I—oh, God!"

Snatching up her beach bag, Angela fled to the house, her face burning. Like a fool, she had completely given herself away!

Once safely in her room, she sank into a chair, feeling miserable and stupid, berating herself a thousand times for letting Niko trick her like that. He would surely tell Alex, and she was going to have to leave. Now there was no other way out.

It seemed like hours that she sat without moving, wondering what to say to Stephanie. Angela had let her own feelings overcome her concern for Crista and Miki. Now she would have to go, and they would think that yet another adult had failed them.

Stephanie appeared at her door. "What are you doing here, in the dark? Can I talk to you for a minute?" Without waiting for a reply, Stephanie flung herself onto the bed. "I had a terrible argument with Niko early this afternoon over Petra. We nearly broke off the engagement. I've never seen him so angry. That viper has the whole house hypnotized."

Angela, about to blurt out that she was planning to leave, bit her tongue. Stephanie was too upset over her argument with Niko, and this was not the moment to add to her anguish.

After a cooling shower, Angela found her Greek dress washed and ironed by the devoted Maria, and decided to wear it once again. She would never be able to put it on in Springport, and in fact, wouldn't even take it with her.

When Angela came out onto the patio to have an ouzo with Stephanie and Savvas, he said, "You are surely Greek, Angela, descended from Pericles."

Angela felt too miserable to do anything but smile wanly.

"I'd better go and find Niko," said Stephanie at last, rising. "Now we've both cooled off, anyway."

Angela rose as well, not wanting to be alone with Savvas. Just then Yianni called to him to help fix a patio light that wasn't working properly.

Taking advantage of her opportunity, Angela slipped away from the house and sauntered into the garden. She was feeling jumpy and restless, trying to rehearse what she would tell Stephanie the next day. When Angela looked around the garden, she felt an aching in her throat. She would have liked to remain long enough to see the figs and pomegranates ripen. Glancing upward at the sky, she thought it looked like a velvet canopy studded with diamonds.

"A star falls occasionally," a low, vibrant voice said behind her.

Angela jumped, startled and flustered, to see Alex standing there. She noticed that he was wearing a white linen suit and a navy-blue jersey shirt, unbuttoned to the middle of his chest.

"Are you—leaving?" she asked.

"Yes, we're going to Athens for a few days by helicopter."

"We?" It slipped out before she could clamp her lips shut.

"Niko and I."

She flushed deeply, hoping he couldn't discern the relief she felt that it was not Petra he was taking with him.

"I haven't had a chance to thank you for saving my children from a cold and uncomfortable night. You have become their guardian angel, always turning up when you are most needed."

Angela didn't dare to look at him. She was already trembling under his praises.

"Imagine going off like that because of a mangy kitten. I cannot fathom the childish mind. I must bow to your greater experience." He looked steadily at her, making her shiver with longing for him. Never had she seen him look so handsome, or so remote. At the same time that Angela wished to escape from his painful scrutiny she longed to be with him for a precious moment more.

"Uh, the teaching materials you had mentioned. If it isn't too much trouble, we could use some ruled copy paper and soft pencils. . . ." Angela heard herself talking on and on, to her own astonishment. What was she doing? Had she completely lost her mind? She was supposed to be preparing herself to leave Greece. Now she would have her opportunity, with Alex and Niko gone. And yet, perversely, with no Alex to trouble her, might she not remain for a while longer?

161

"Of course I'll bring the material. I wanted to say, Angela, that your teaching methods are enormously successful. Each day the children speak better English. I am impressed, and most grateful to you."

Alex smiled at her, and the smile cut her heart in two. She had a wild impulse to cover his mouth with kisses.

Frightened at her feelings, she turned her back to him and walked a few feet away, breathing deeply.

"Angela? What's wrong?" He came up behind her and touched her arms. Even though the pressure was gentle she could feel his hands burning her flesh through the flimsy sleeves. She stiffened, and as she did so his grip tightened.

Insistently he turned her to face him and stared at her with burning eyes. No longer smiling, he was biting his lower lip savagely, while he held her arms so tightly that his knuckles turned white.

"There's no need for you to—to feel grateful," she whispered, trying to defuse the dangerous tension between them. "Anything I can do for the children gives me more pleasure than it could possibly give you."

"Don't presume to tell me what gives me pleasure," he said, so low she had to strain to hear him. "I will tell you. Better still, I will show you."

He pulled her into his arms forcefully, while her heart stopped and such fear gripped her that she tried to fend him off by putting her palms flat against his chest. She could feel his heart pounding against her fingers.

"No," she whispered. "No."

"Never say no to me," he hissed, drawing her closer to him in such a crushing embrace that she felt he would crack all the bones in her body. Insistently his mouth sought hers and assaulted it with a kiss so

162

hard, so angry, she could only save herself from pain by going completely limp in his arms.

Her lips parted and her body softly accepted his hard one, straining powerfully against her. Almost in a trance, she slid her arms around his neck.

Alex kissed her again and again, his hand, tangled in her hair, pulling her head back, the look in his eye wild.

Angela felt her control ebbing as she returned his kisses with every ounce of love within her. Moments later he moved his burning lips to her throat, while his fingers reached upward from her waist and explored the curves of her firm, voluptuous breasts. She gasped and pressed closer to him, her response triggering his ardor.

Angela felt as if she'd been lifted up to the stars, so heavenly was his embrace. She was sinking, weakening, longing to surrender totally.

Suddenly Petra's image broke into her ecstasy. Alex was engaged to Petra, and that thought gave her the strength to draw back abruptly.

Perhaps Alex had also remembered Petra, or else read Angela's mind as was his wont. He released her, whispering, "Angela, Angela," as if it pained him to say her name.

Unable to utter a word, Angela turned and rushed away.

Chapter Eleven

The next ten days were a welcome respite for Angela, even though she couldn't stop thinking about Alex for more than moments at a time. At least she might walk through the olive grove or the garden without fearing that he would turn up unexpectedly. Nor was Niko there to torment her.

Angela spent much of her time with Stephanie, and they resumed their affectionate, close friendship as in the old days. Stephanie accepted Angela's announcement of the broken engagement with sympathy and silence. In gratitude Angela had decided to say nothing to Stephanie about Niko after all. It was obvious that his advances to her had been made out of spite and hostility, as well as to unnerve her. Anyway, she was planning to go home.

Home. Whenever she thought of it Angela felt depressed. Springport would never be the same for her. To take up her old life in the small town again seemed terribly unappealing. There would be no more Rory—except, perhaps, as Nancy's husband—and there wasn't another man in town Angela would even have considered dating. The truth was that no man she knew—or could imagine meeting—would ever compare with Alex. A hundred times she relived their last meeting in the garden, and the way he had kissed her. Had any woman in the world ever been kissed like that?

Every nuance of their embrace returned to haunt her: the wild look in his eye, the exquisite pressure of his fingers, his ravenous hunger for her. It made no sense, none at all.

Had Niko told him anything? No, it couldn't be. Alex had not behaved with love but with anger, with an insistence upon having something forbidden to him. There had been a desperate quality to his embrace. The truth was, surely, that he was pledged to marry Petra but Angela attracted him to some extent, and Greek men didn't stint their pleasures. Besides, Niko has probably been filling Alex's head with stories about her, implying that she was immoral and unprincipled in every respect. . . . And hadn't she returned kiss for kiss, almost as if to support Niko's accusations?

"Angela, where are the children?" Stephanie asked in alarm. The friends were lying on the beach, reading. Angela sat up and shaded her eyes with her hand. "There, near the rocks."

Stephanie squinted. "They're too close to Petra. Miki! Crista!" Stephanie yelled, waving them back.

Ever since the children had run away Stephanie had seen to it that Petra was never alone with them, and the children cooperated fully. They imitated their aunt and screwed up their faces when Petra went by, refusing to speak to her. Savvas, too, ignored Petra. Angela noticed that Mrs. Pallas, and even her husband, seemed much less friendly to the woman than formerly.

Watching Petra now, Angela had a momentary flicker of sympathy for her. Never vengeful, Angela found it difficult to understand the harsh, unforgiving ways of the Greeks. Savvas and Stephanie were two of the kindest people on earth, but when it came to Petra they had turned to stone. Of course, Angela realized that some of her own sympathy toward her rival was occasioned by guilt. Alex was engaged to Petra, and Angela had no right to want him, no right to love him so deeply, or to let him embrace her when the whim took him.

Without troubling to dissect all her motives, Angela was trying to be fair to Petra. In vain she had timidly ventured to defend her to Stephanie and Savvas—or at least take into account the pressures Petra had been under, the blow her pride had suffered when Alex had originally rejected her. Besides, loving Alex as she did herself, Angela could identify with any other woman who loved him.

"Are you kidding?" Savvas had squealed derisively. "I never liked Petra before. Now, when she has shown me her true colors, now that I see she could take out her anger on innocent children—no! Finished!" Savvas had brushed his hands smartly together as if cleansing them of impurities.

Angela now walked to the water's edge where Petra was gathering shells. "I wish we could be more friendly to each other, Petra. I'm sure you didn't really mean any harm when you told the children—"

Petra recoiled from Angela, a look of fury distorting her features. "How do you dare talk to me, you of all people! You're all in it together, you and Stephanie and Savvas! Do you think I don't know why you came here, why you're ingratiating yourselves with Alex's brats?" Petra's eyes blazed, and Angela quailed as she saw the angry woman come toward her menacingly.

As Angela hastily backed away Petra laughed harshly, her expression turning to one of disdain. "Never mind, Angelamou," she mimicked nastily, "your plan has failed. Alex is in Athens making the final arrangements for our wedding. In two weeks it will all be over. Oh, don't worry. You won't have to leave. It would be practical for you to stay on and take care of the brats while Alex and I are on our honeymoon."

Tossing her head, Petra laughed, watching with pleasure as the color drained from her rival's face. Then Petra walked triumphantly down the beach.

Angela couldn't remember how she passed the next couple of hours. There was a heavy weight on her chest, an ache in her throat. She could hardly remember a time when she had not been on this island, madly, hopelessly in love with Alex Pallas. In spite of Petra's horrible words Angela kept thinking of the way Alex had embraced her. Could a man about to be married to one woman kiss another as he had kissed her? She shut her eyes in an agony of despair, feeling again those powerful arms pinning her fragile body to his, and those hard, persistent kisses. . . .

Remember, he is Greek, Angela told herself. Hadn't Niko, who loved Stephanie, tried to embrace her? Angela was simply out of her league. She was no match for these dominant men of vast experience. She'd had no business getting into such an appalling predicament. Her one means of extricating herself was to flee like a thief.

Angela finally made her way to her room and picked up her Greek grammar. She simply had to divert herself from her obsession. She didn't stop to ask herself why she should be studying a language for which she would soon have no further use. Now that she could read simple words and sentences, and could make some sense of the grammar, her progress was remarkably swift.

Sitting on the patio, she was so absorbed in her book, repeating phrases aloud to herself, that she didn't notice that Mrs. Pallas had joined her and was seated only a few feet away.

"No, my child," the woman said, smiling. She corrected Angela's pronunciation.

Angela reddened self-consciously. "It is so difficult," she said in Greek.

"But you are doing very well," Mrs. Pallas replied "Sigá, sigá, slowly. You understand what I say now?"

"A little," Angela confirmed shyly.

"Good. Listen carefully. I am pleased to be able to tell you myself what your visit means to me, to my husband, and to the little ones. Always I have known you must be an angel, like your name says. You have been so kind to my Stephanie. You have given her so much. You understand me?"

Angela nodded, terribly embarrassed. "I also received much. Stephanie is my closest friend. Her joy in life has—has—" Angela halted, as Greek words failed her.

"Never mind, I understand." Mrs. Pallas smiled at Angela, reminding her acutely of Alex. "You like it here, my child?"

"Oh, yes, it is the most beautiful place in the world," Angela replied rashly, falling into the manner of Greek hyperbole. Still, although she might not have been everywhere else in the world, she was sure nothing could affect her the way this island did, especially when she couldn't disassociate it from Alex.

"Would you like to stay in Greece? Would you miss your homeland very much?"

Angela hesitated and dropped her eyes from the woman's kindly but shrewd gaze. What was she hinting at? Was she thinking of Savvas?

Mrs. Pallas was clearly waiting for an answer, her intelligent eyes fixed patiently on Angela's face.

"I would like to stay here but, of course, I would also wish to visit my sister very often," Angela said

168

carefully. It was as close to the truth as she dared to tell. Something about Mrs. Pallas prevented her from being more evasive.

"Of course," agreed Mrs. Pallas with complacency. "Your sister could visit you here for as long as she wished. Tell me, my child, you are not going to marry that man in America, are you?"

Angela turned crimson, her color preventing her from pretending not to have understood the question. She shook her head slowly, eyes down, hating her blushes that always gave her feelings away.

After a silence Mrs. Pallas deftly changed the subject. "My grandchildren, they are like Stephanie and Savvas at the same age," she remarked, looking away from Angela's burning cheeks.

"Yes," Angela murmured, "it is so easy to love them."

"But they have no mother," sighed Mrs. Pallas, suddenly turning to look intently at Angela again. "I worry very much for them."

Angela dropped her eyes and was silent. She, too, worried about the children, but what could she say after Petra's earlier assurance that she and Alex were to be married? Was Mrs. Pallas trying to tell Angela, somewhat obliquely, that Petra, Alex's wife or not, would never be a mother to the children? Did Mrs. Pallas wish, in fact, that Angela would remain in Greece as a teacher for them?

"What is all this gloom?" Savvas came out onto the patio and made the two women a mock bow. "It is a beautiful afternoon and nobody has died that I know of, so why the funeral faces? Come, Manulamou," he said happily to his mother, kissing her on both cheeks. "Let's be happy."

Mrs. Pallas looked indulgently at her son, and then

169

rose. "I will see to the dinner. You, Savvas, should spend more time with your father. He has much to teach you about the business—"

"Yes, yes," Savvas answered impatiently, focusing his attention on Angela as soon as his mother's back was turned. "I will take you for a sail in our little boat."

"No, not now, please, Savvas—"

Ignoring her objections, Savvas clapped his peaked fisherman's cap on her head and led her, protesting, down to the beach. "You have been avoiding me, Angela, and I won't have it. It's not often I have you to myself, without my interfering brother always keeping tabs on me."

Angela's heart lurched at the mention of Alex, and the aching returned to clutch at her chest. She could already see Petra in a white wedding dress, Alex standing tall and unbearably handsome at her side, smiling at her. . . .

"Here's the boat," Savvas said, pointing to the three-foot oval fiberglass boat with a single mast, tied near a rock.

Angela looked at it in disbelief. "This is what you meant? I thought it was a toy for the children. You aren't serious about sailing her?"

"Of course I am. Oh, I know Alex and Niko sneer at my sailing ability, but the test is a sailfish like this, not that big monster. Here I either do it right or wrong. It's not a matter of opinion, because if you make a mistake—oops! Out you go."

"Some other time, please, Savvas. I'm tired, and it looks as if it's going to be rough out there."

"Nonsense. There isn't a cloud in the sky, and the sun is as hot as ever."

"But I feel a wind starting."

"Pah, it is nothing. It may get worse later, but by

170

then you'll be asleep in your little bed. We'll be back in an hour, I promise you."

"That will give us very little time to change for dinner, and we'll be late—"

Savvas shook her by the shoulder. "Stop it; stop spoiling all my fun. My exacting brother isn't here to play the tryrant. Nobody will lock the door if we come in a couple of minutes late. Unfortunately Alex returns late tonight."

Angela turned her head at that news so that Savvas wouldn't see her perturbed expression. She felt so flustered that she waded out to the boat with Savvas after all.

"You sit here, Angela, and be careful which way you lean."

Angela was amazed at how quickly the little boat skimmed over the foaming waves. But she became anxious as the wind increased and the sea became rougher within minutes.

"Savvas, I don't like this. I think there's going to be a storm. Please, let's go back now."

Savvas opened his mouth to say something when all of a sudden his eyes widened in astonishment. He muttered in Greek and fumbled nervously with the sail.

Turning to see what was upsetting Savvas, Angela grew frightened at the sight of a large, angry wave bearing down on them.

"Stay calm, stay calm. When I tell you, lean back as far as you can, but don't fall off, of course." His quavering voice made the attempt at a joke seem feeble.

Angela shut her eyes and did as she was told. She felt the flat boat rise sharply on the wave and then fall crazily on the other side, causing a fluttering in her stomach.

"Savvas, please! We must go back!"

"With pleasure, only the wind has turned. Quick, lean to the port!"

They averted another disaster. By now Angela was terribly alarmed. She remembered that Savvas was an indifferent sailor, and she had never been in such a flimsy boat, and certainly not in this kind of sea. The tiny vessel was swirling in the angry waters as if it were made of paper.

"We're going back, don't worry," said Savvas in a very strained voice.

They had left the beach far behind and were now quite close to Rocky Point. The sky had turned black, and lightning was flashing dangerously near them.

Angela stared at the jutting volcanic rocks with growing anxiety. "Do we have to go so close?" she queried Savvas.

"Yes, or risk getting carried out to sea. If only we can get around the point and over to the other side. The rocks are a little softer there."

If she hadn't been so scared, Angela might have laughed. As it was, Savvas barely had control of the boat, which was tossing like a plaything.

There was now a howling wind, and both of them were drenched. Angela saw clearly that one false move and the boat was going to tip over and dump them into the churning sea. Suddenly there was a terrific crack of thunder.

A second later they crashed against a rock. She heard the horrible sound of splitting wood as the mast broke and the sail flapped wildly and cascaded into the water.

Angela was blinded by the foaming, sputtering waves. She reached out without seeing and grabbed a sharp rock, holding on with both hands, terrified, while the swelling waters tried to tear her from her anchor. The rain was pelting down in sheets.

"Savvas, Savvas," she screamed. For several moments she hung on, feeling the waves wash completely over her again and again. This was going to be it, the end of everything.

After what seemed an eternity, there was a lull and the waters momentarily receded. Opening her eyes, in spite of the way they were stinging from the salt, Angela could see that she was only a few feet from some flat, solid-looking rocks. If only she could swim to them. She feared, however, to let go and try because her aching legs indicated that there was a dangerous undertow, and she might be carried out to sea in one burst.

Angela clung to her perch, immobilized by fear. Where was Savvas? He had vanished, and Angela began to call his name hysterically. Her cries, however, were immediately borne away on the relentless wind lashing the sea against the rocks.

Angela suddenly grew calm. She could do nothing for Savvas with her yelling. Better to save her strength and try to swim to the flat rocks. Savvas was a strong swimmer himself.

Taking a deep breath, she let go and plunged toward her destination, kicking her legs with every remaining ounce of strength. Several times she reached out, straining for the flat rock, only to be pushed back each time by the roaring water.

Fight, fight, don't give in, she told herself desperately as she was twisted as if in a whirlpool. Just then, by some quirk, a wave came from the other side and delivered her neatly onto the very rocks she had been trying so hard to reach.

Breathlessly, with her last effort, she pulled herself up higher, temporarily out of reach of the menacing waves which continued to crash around her ankles. She lay back exhausted.

When Angela was finally able to sit up and take stock, she saw that her sundress hung in shreds over her bikini and that her hands were cut and bleeding.

"Angela," she heard weakly from behind her.

"Savvas! Here!" She reached down and extended her hand.

Savvas grabbed her arm and slowly, painfully, pulled himself up, collapsing beside her. "I've hurt my leg and broken my wrist, I think," he murmured, his face very pale.

Angela tore her dress to make a sling and gently bandaged his wrist, which was already swollen and discolored. "It will be all right, as soon as we get you back to a doctor—"

"Never mind. I deserve it. It's all my fault. I should have realized—"

"Shh, don't talk about it now. Just rest. We're safe." For the time being, she amended silently. If the unpredictable waters should rise, they would be washed away from their sanctuary.

Fortunately the storm ended as suddenly as it had begun. It grew very dark, and soon a quarter moon appeared as well as a million stars, which were reflected in the black waters.

"I'm so hungry," Angela said, giggling nervously. She felt giddy and light-headed, and thought she might have a slight fever.

Savvas came closer and put his good arm around her. She could see that he was in pain because of his wrist, but he refused to acknowledge it or even talk about it. "I'm so sorry, Angelamou. I am everything Alex says I am—stupid and irresponsible. But no more. You'll see. As soon as we get home I will turn over a new leaf and become such a solid citizen that you'll be proud of me. And I'll take wonderful care of you when you are my wife."

Angela stiffened under his arm.

"What is it? You're still angry with me? I don't blame you, but as soon as we are rescued you will love me again, Angelamou."

He bent his head over hers. Their hair was wet and sticky with salt, and they were so cold, even huddled together, that their teeth began to chatter.

"Savvas," she implored, "you must stop talking this way, even jokingly. I can never marry you, never."

Savvas moved away from her and said sulkily, "Why not? Still that silly lawyer across the ocean?"

Angela paused, and then slowly shook her head.

"Ah! I knew it. Always I knew you didn't care for him. But then why—"

"Please, Savvas, no more questions, they're too painful." She bowed her head, the misery of her feelings adding to her physical discomfort.

For several moments Savvas silently scrutinized her features. "You're in love with Alex, aren't you?"

The blunt question took her by surprise, and she involuntarily cringed as if she'd been dealt a blow. Keeping her head down, she remained silent.

"So," Savvas snorted, "that's a pretty mess. But now I understand. I understand everything. I've had my suspicions, but I couldn't believe that a beauty like you would ever dream of—Oh, what's the use. You know, of course, that it's hopeless. Alex will marry Petra this time. She has him bewitched, that woman. She *is* a witch, I think."

Savvas absent-mindedly ran his fingers through his tangled hair. " What do you see in that egotistical brother of mine, anyway?"

"He—he reminds me of Apollo," Angela answered idiotically.

"*Po, po, po!*" exclaimed Savvas, stroking the air with his good hand. "As bad as that, eh?" He sighed.

175

"I won't say I'm not disappointed that you'd rather be my sister than my wife. But my poor little Angela, what will you do?"

Disappointed Savvas might be, but not devastated, Angela noted. His feeling for her was merely a passing infatuation, and she was relieved, since she had no wish to hurt him.

"What will you do?" he asked her again.

"Nothing," she answered flatly. "There's nothing I can do except go home. Petra told me—she said that Alex—that they were going to be married within two weeks—" Angela halted, as her throat closed up.

"Pooh! Alex is the stupidest man on earth. But never mind, Angela, you will meet a hundred better than him who would give anything in the world to have you. Don't shake your head. You will, you'll see. I myself fall in love every few months, and each time I think it will last forever—"

"I have no doubt that you do," Angela said dryly. "But I am not like you."

"Then what, Angela? You will mourn forever? Never marry at all, is that what you mean? Pah, I don't believe it for a minute. That is plain silly. You can't love Alex that much."

"Savvas, please," Angela implored, her voice breaking.

"Tsk. I personally will kidnap Petra and carry her off to a faraway land so that she is never seen again. Wait, maybe I can marry her myself, as Stephanie suggested. Eh, I would hate it, of course. I'd feel as if I was chewing a lemon for the rest of my life. But if it would make you happy—"

"Oh, please, stop, Savvas," begged Angela, whose tears now turned to hysterical laughter. She was giddy, and felt an overwhelming sense of relief at having told the truth to somebody at last.

176

After a while they ceased to speak. The wind turned even colder and they could concentrate on nothing but keeping warm.

"If we can remain awake and moving, we'll be all right," Savvas said softly, licking his dry lips. "Surely by morning—"

"Savvas! Isn't that a light on the water?"

"You're right! And I can hear the motor. Here we are! Help! Shout, Angela, shout!"

She joined her cries to his, and the light and sound drew nearer. It was a speedboat, and in it was Niko.

"How did you get here?" asked Savvas. "Is—is Alex back also?"

Niko, glaring at Savvas, cut the motor.

"Anyhow, it took you long enough," Savvas said with feigned nonchalance, trying to control his chattering teeth.

"Shut up, you fool," Niko snapped. "Come, Angela," he said, helping her into the boat. He wrapped a blanket around her shivering body, and she was surprised that there was no hostility in his behavior toward her.

"You are all right?" Niko asked, searching her face with what seemed to be a sympathetic expression.

"Yes, but Savvas has broken his wrist and—"

"Never mind about him," Niko interrupted. He extended a Thermos of hot coffee.

Angela was so exhausted that she huddled in her blanket and sipped her coffee, a lethargy stealing over her.

Savvas, also wrapped in a blanket, had recovered all his bravado. "I didn't expect you back until much later tonight."

"It *is* later tonight, fool. It's past midnight. Alex could see there was going to be a storm, and we took off early."

177

"Alex," Savvas said with scorn. "Naturally, Alex sees all, knows all. Where is he?"

Niko snorted. "I left him making some adjustments to the helicopter. When he returns to the house and finds out what has happened, he will murder you. What were you thinking of, to go off in that thing? Not a living creature was astir this afternoon, everyone says so. The whole world knew there would be a storm except you." Suddenly glancing at Angela, Niko switched to Greek.

She was too tired to follow the conversation and dozed off for a few minutes, awakening and hearing snatches. "Your fishing cap came to shore, and Petra brought it back—"

"She would!"

"Shut up, Savvas, and listen. You have caused a terrible commotion, and if your parents don't recover, it will be your fault. Stephanie wanted to come after you herself in the storm, and only by locking her in her room was your father able to prevent it. He has taken to his bed, your mother's face is the color of whitewash, the children are screaming for Angela . . ."

Angela simply couldn't keep awake, and her heavy lids closed over her eyes.

The next thing she knew, she was being lifted out of the boat by a pair of powerful arms and carried tenderly up from the beach. She could tell it was Alex without opening her eyes. Too exhausted to pretend, she put her arms around his neck gratefully and leaned against him.

He was murmuring into her ear in Greek, but she was too sleepy to make an effort to understand. It was the last time she would be in Alex's arms, and there she nestled, banishing everything else from her consciousness.

Chapter Twelve

Angela awoke as the sun caressed her face with its warmth. Her clock said ten-thirty. Sitting up slowly, she hugged her knees. Her limbs were sore from the battle with the sea, but otherwise she felt remarkably clearheaded.

She remembered with a pang all of the previous day's events: Petra's devastating news, the sail with Savvas, the wrecking of the small boat, the struggle to survive, her confession to Savvas, their rescue by a strangely gentle Niko, and finally being carried home in the arms of her beloved.

A sudden feeling of misery assailed Angela. She knew what she had to do, and it must be today.

There was a knock at the door and smiling, bright-eyed Stephanie poked her head into the room. "I've brought you breakfast myself. Everyone has been wanting to come in here: the children, my mother. Savvas is still asleep, of course, and I can't find Niko or Alex anywhere. I thought you'd want to drink your coffee and comb your hair before facing the world."

Stephanie set down the tray and embraced Angela. "I can't tell you how relieved I am, Ange, that you're all right, no thanks to my crazy brother. We were so frantic when Petra came up from the beach carrying Savvas's cap. And my father locked me in my room. I felt so helpless, looking out at that terrible storm and worrying about you. Then Niko came back and apparently rushed down to look for you in the speedboat. Mother was hysterical and I was afraid Papa would have a stroke. I could hear the children screaming. When Alex got back, I thought he'd take charge calmly as usual. Instead I heard him yelling and behaving as frantically as everyone else. Apparently by the time Alex got down to the beach, Niko had rescued both of you. Oh, listen to me, talking on and on. Tell me, how do you feel?"

Angela took a deep breath and had a sip of coffee. "I'm all right, I guess," she replied, her voice sounding strangely hollow to her own ears. "Stephanie, I want you to help me. Promise me, as my dearest friend, that you will do as I ask."

Stephanie's smile froze on her face when she saw that Angela was deadly serious. "But—"

"No buts. Listen. I must get away from the island today. By helicopter, as that is quickest. While I pack, I want you to go to Niko and ask him to take me to Athens. No questions, no reasons. He'll understand. It is important that I leave here as soon as possible, and that nobody know until I am gone. Bring two donkeys to the olive grove—"

Stephanie clasped her trembling hands tightly and looked in bewilderment at Angela. "Why can't you tell me what happened? It must have to do with Savvas, I know it must. Surely you know you can trust me. Whatever it is, whatever has happened, I'd do anything in the world for you. Even though it will hurt me to have you go like this, when you had promised to stay on. . . ." Stephanie's eyes grew moist with tears.

Angela embraced her, trying to keep her own tears back. "I'll write you as soon as I get—home. I'll tell

180

you everything then. By that time it won't matter. The most important thing, Steph, is to make sure the children are far away so that they won't see me leave—"

"But what can I say to everyone?"

"Say I'm exhausted and will be sleeping all day."

Stephanie, now crying openly, nodded, staring miserably at her friend. She had never seen Angela look more beautiful, or more tragic, her hair curling onto her shoulders, her violet-blue eyes so sad, peering tearfully through her thick, golden lashes, her red lips trembling.

"Please, Stephanie," Angela begged.

"All right. But what if Niko refuses—"

"He won't. He's been wanting to get rid of me from the start, you know he has."

To that Stephanie had no answer, and she slipped out of the room.

It took Angela very little time to pack her belongings. Then she had a quick shower and dressed. Still Stephanie had not appeared in the olive grove with the donkeys.

Angela grew worried. It would soon be time for lunch, and everyone would be practically outside her window on the patio. What was taking Stephanie so long?

Angela wondered if something had gone wrong. She had meant to put her bags on one donkey and ride the other to the helicopter port. But time passed and no Stephanie. Instead, various members of the family gathered for lunch. Although Angela tried not to look out, she couldn't help herself. When she saw the children hopping up and down, shouting to each other and behaving like their normally energetic selves, her resolve nearly evaporated. Savvas was bending over hs plate, his merry face quite subdued. She could imagine

181

what criticism he had had to endure because of his misadventure. Those absent from the table were Stephanie, Petra, Niko, and Alex.

Angela began to pace up and down, her agitation growing with every second. She simply could not bear to be so close to the children and decided to sneak out with her bags and make her way to the olive grove to wait for Stephanie. She set down her suitcases and leaned against her favorite olive tree, her hand caressing the familiar knotty trunk. The thought of wrenching herself from the island, from the children, from Stephanie, was very painful. And yet it would be more painful to remain there to watch Alex and Petra make their final wedding plans, especially when Savvas and Niko knew how she felt about Alex. She would sooner die than stay, under the circumstances.

Angela looked at her watch. She would give Stephanie five minutes more and then make her way on foot to the helicopter. At least nobody would think of looking for her in the olive grove.

There Angela was mistaken. Someone approached within a few feet of her. Was it Stephanie? Angela jumped as she heard footsteps crackling on the dry twigs.

From the way the bottom dropped out of her stomach, and her heart began to pound, Angela knew even before she looked up that it had to be Alex.

For a moment she didn't move. Neither did he. Silently they stood still, staring at each other across the clearing. After eleven days of being parted from him, Angela saw that the sight of him still played havoc with her respiration.

Alex came slowly toward her, a look of burning intensity in his eyes. When he was almost upon her, he halted. "So this is how you repay our hospitality! You wish to go off without one word, and in fact get

182

my own sister to assist you in making your escape."
His tone was bitter, his words clipped. An errant
muscle was flickering in his cheek.

Stephanie had failed to keep her word! Angela's
face grew even hotter, and she knew she was blushing
fiercely. She wished it were possible for her to sink into
the earth right there and be covered by a carpet of
shiny green olives.

"I—I only want to do what is best," Angela whispered in a voice so weak that Alex had to bend forward to hear her. "I've made a terrible mess of everything. It's all my fault, and now I want to leave as
quickly and as quietly as possible. I would have written—"

"Indeed!" he snapped derisively. "And what of my
father, who has opened his home to you? And my
mother, who looks upon you as a daughter? How
about my children, who may never quite recover from
such treachery? And my sister, who is so upset at being
unable to help you that she is ashamed to face you?
I'll leave my foolish brother out of it, because he deserves no consideration after he nearly lost you yesterday. I thought you had greater courage, Angela, than
to sneak away without a word of good-bye."

Angela lowered her face from his scorching eyes, but
she could still hear his voice and, as always, it made
her ache for him.

"And what of me?" Alex's voice grew husky. "I do
not even know what is going on in my own house. I
have to learn from Niko that you have broken your
engagement, from Savvas that it may have something
to do with me, and finally from Stephanie that you're
proposing to run away from the island without even
a word to me."

With every second Angela's mortification increased.
He knew everything! And how angry he was with her!

183

Suddenly she felt his hands on her own, sending a frightening tremor through her. Insistently he held them. "Tell me yourself, Angela, anything you have to tell me," he said gruffly.

Her eyes swimming in sudden tears, she focused on his face imploringly. "Why make me speak when you know—when you know—everything?"

"No, Angela, I don't know anything. I want to hear it from you."

"Please don't force me to say something that—that pains me greatly," she whispered, lowering her head, as the tears began to roll slowly down her cheeks.

Reaching into his pocket, Alex took out a crisply laundered handkerchief and handed it to her. "For someone who sheds so many tears, you are remarkably unprepared to deal with them."

Angela dabbed at her face, furious with herself, and with him. "It is only since—since coming here—I never cry, usually—" A fresh watering prevented further speech.

Fool, idiot, she berated herself, trying desperately to stem the flow. This was what she had wished to avoid. His mocking tone, his cool arrogance. No doubt it pleased him to have her so completely in his power.

"Once you tell me everything yourself, Angela, and listen to what I have to say, I promise you can go where you will." The muscle in his cheek was twitching once again.

Angela tried but nothing was forthcoming. "I—I can't. Oh, please, Alex, let me go!" she implored. "You have no right to—to—"

"I have every right," he said softly, his eyes taking on the dangerously intense look that turned her blood to water in her veins. "S'agapó, Angela," he murmured.

Her heart lurched, and she felt herself teetering.

Surely she had misheard him. Surely he hadn't told her that he loved her!

Glancing quickly at him, she could see a barely concealed hunger in his expression, and his eyes continued to probe her face with the searing power of a laser beam.

"Do you love *me*? You must tell me the truth," Alex said slowly in Greek.

Angela swallowed, hardly able to follow what was happening. What did it matter what she said, since in any event he was going to marry Petra. If she told him how she felt, might he not just wish, in his Greek way, to have his cake and eat it too—before she left and he lost his chance forever?

"Is it Savvas that you love?" The question came out taut, uncertain. "Every time I have turned around, there you have been with my brother—" Alex chewed his lip and halted. "He says it isn't true, but I don't believe him. I want to hear it from you."

"I'm—I'm fond of Savvas, of course. But it is only a sisterly affection," Angela whispered. "Oh, if only I had left here weeks ago!" she cried.

"Why didn't you?" Alex asked, his voice soft again.

"Because of the children. I could see that Petra didn't care for them, nor they for her. I thought if I stayed on for a little while, made them see how lovable they were, and that it wasn't their fault that Petra didn't want them—Oh, I don't know what I thought! I was so foolish. Even your mother realizes. She hinted that I might—I might stay here and teach them, even after—after your wedding."

"Is that what you think?" Alex smiled suddenly, a smile that so pained Angela that it brought tears to her eyes once more.

"What wedding are you speaking of?" he then asked, frowning.

"Yours and Petra's of course," Angela whispered. "She told me she was going to marry you within two weeks—"

"Ah! And Petra is, as you well know, the very soul of honesty," he said scornfully. He paused. "There are no plans for a wedding that I know of. Not at the moment."

Angela stared at him. He was looking coolly amused, and Angela was determined to finish her story so that he would let her go quickly. "Obviously I have to leave because the situation is intolerable. The children have been put in danger because of me. Savvas has had false hopes, and I wasn't able to convince him of the truth until yesterday. Stephanie and Niko have quarreled because of me—"

"And what did you think my feelings were in all this?" he asked her gruffly. "Do you think I kiss every woman as I kissed you?"

"I—I wouldn't know," Angela whispered, her heart lurching at the thought of Alex kissing Petra.

"Why didn't you tell me you'd broken your engagement?"

"I didn't think it would concern you, that it would change anything, when you are engaged to Petra—"

"Why didn't you tell me that she lured the children from Rocky Point? That she threatened to drown that kitten? That she was such a dangerous influence?"

"You didn't want to hear it, that's why. Savvas and Stephanie told you—"

"Never mind them. I'm asking you, Angela. Why have you never trusted me enough to tell me anything?"

Angela paused and lowered her eyes before whispering, "Because I haven't trusted myself to be near you."

186

"I want you near me now," he murmured, taking her tenderly in his arms. He kissed her forehead, her cheeks, and finally her lips with such unexpected gentleness that the tears once more gathered in her eyes. As he stroked her tangled hair he murmured into her ear, "*S'agapó polí.* I love you very much. Don't you understand it yet?"

Angela couldn't think, couldn't understand anything. Alex desired her, perhaps, but he was going to marry Petra. And yet, all her resolution and control had evaporated under his incredibly tender embrace, and she leaned weakly against him and hid her face in his shirt. The unbidden tears flowed once more.

"Angelika, don't cry so, *agápi mu.* You told Savvas that you're going to be a spinster. Is that true?"

"Yes," she sobbed.

"What? This hair not to have a man's fingers entwined in its silken strands, like this? That exquisite form to do without a man's caresses?" he continued huskily, running his hand lightly down to her slender waist. "Those lips not to sweeten some man's days and make him impatient for the nights?" He kissed her long and tenderly once again.

Angela, with her last ounce of willpower, pushed against his chest with her hands. "Yes, yes!"

"That's right, Angelika, always say yes to me."

"I mean no!" she corrected, becoming flustered. How could she think at all when her longing for him was causing her acute physical pain. "Please stop, Alex, please!" she begged.

"Very well." He stepped back from her abruptly, and then he smiled.

"You're only playing with me!" she accused him, her eyes blazing.

"No, Angela, I am not. Be careful not to grow so angry. I like my woman sweet-tempered."

"In that case you're in for a disappointment," she snapped, thinking of the icy, spiteful Petra.

"I think not, my sweet angel, I think not."

"You *are* playing with me, now you know—everything. Just let me go, please. You can laugh at my foolishness when I am far from here. You and Petra can make a big joke of it—"

Alex's face darkened suddenly, and he grabbed her arm in an iron grip. "Don't you dare speak like that to me, damn you! When you stepped off that plane, I knew I was done for! Stephanie had been praising you to the skies for years. I knew about the intelligence, the kindness, the warmth, the fine character. But I didn't really expect it to come wrapped up in such breathtaking beauty."

Angela stared at him, wide-eyed.

"Believe me, if I could have put you back on the plane, I would have done so. Because if ever I have had an idea of the woman I wanted for the rest of my life, there she was walking toward me in the airport. But she had a fiancé in America."

"But Petra—"

"Yes, of course, always Petra. The reason that Niko can't take you to Athens in the helicopter is that he is on his way there with Petra. It is finished between us."

Alex pulled Angela into his arms again, but this time without gentleness. He crushed her to him, kissing her hungrily. His hands explored her body insistently, pulling her blouse out of her skirt and unhooking her bra. As he caressed her perfect breasts he looked at her with such an expression of wild adoration that she was left with no doubt that he loved her.

"Oh, Alex!" she cried.

He lifted his face, a look of touching vulnerability there. "Will you say it, please, Angelika?"

"*S'agapó,* Alécco," she whispered. "*S'agapó poli.*"

Again they embraced, and she strained against him, loving him desperately.

Suddenly he released her and held her firmly back from him, blinking his eyes and taking deep breaths. "All right, I've done. Now, do you still wish to leave me?" His voice was gruff, but his eyes glowed with love.

Angela's head was still spinning, and her heart missed every second beat. "When you say it's finished between you and Petra—"

"Finished means finished. I'll admit that for a little while I was going to honor my family's promise, in spite of my love for you. I felt I owed Petra something, and the tragedy with Caterina had shamed me. Besides, it seemed so hopeless to think that you could ever return my feelings. And it's true that Niko had talked against you from the beginning. He knows me well and saw immediately that I'd been bowled over by you. He feared you were a fortune hunter, unscrupulous, and that you were after Savvas. He didn't want me to make a fool of myself. I tried to argue with him, but underneath I felt he was right—at least about my hopeless love—especially as every time I saw you with my brother, he was kissing you, or you were laughing together. Savvas is young, handsome, without a care. Why should you not prefer him? Then I remembered your engagement, and I wondered if Niko weren't possibly correct."

"It was my fault, Alex, for waiting so long to break the engagement. But Petra—"

"Oh, God, I've never cared for Petra. That was why I refused her in the first place. In fact, I never cared much for Caterina either. I married her on impulse, and out of spite. I was young and stupid, and have

189

paid the penalty, believe me. You are the first woman I have ever loved, Angelika, and will be the last, even if you run away from me now."

"Perhaps I won't run away," Angela said, a beautiful smile transfiguring her face. "Perhaps you'll be able to persuade me to remain."

His eyes narrowed dangerously but he stood well back from her, as if finding it difficult to keep from touching her. "I do owe you an apology," he said, "for ever having doubted your honesty. But believing it was hopeless. I was trying hard to find reasons not to love you. Forgive me, Angelika. The difficulty was that I kept wanting you more and more. God, how I've wanted you! I knew I should let you leave at the end of July, and yet I did everything I could think of to make you stay. I even danced for you in Mykonos, hoping you'd see, that you'd come to love me somehow. Later, when the children ran away, I confronted Petra privately. She broke down and admitted everything. It was then that I felt I could release myself from my promise, and I told her that I could never marry her. She refused to accept that. It was Niko, the meddler, who brought things to a head. He is relentless. He had the story from the children and then backed Petra against the wall. All her animosity spilled forth, and she admitted having taken a letter from your room—" Alex broke off and regarded Angela thoughtfully. "I don't expect you to have much sympathy for Petra."

"I do, a little. I even tried to be friends with her, because she seemed so isolated from everyone. It was then that she told me you were in Athens arranging the wedding."

"My darling Angelika, of the understanding heart. I was, in fact, in Athens convincing Leonidas to disassociate his daughter's marriage from our business venture. He signed the agreement after all, for considerable financial gain, I might add. Niko had come with me. I told him I could never marry Petra, and that I loved you to distraction. It was only then that Niko told me he'd tricked you into revealing your broken engagement. He'd begun to believe that your feelings for the children were genuine—and perhaps for me, too.

"As for Petra, there is a man in Athens who has been mooning around her for years. I think she would quite like him if she stopped to consider him and forgot about me. I don't believe it's love for me as much as stubbornness, a wish to salvage her injured pride. Then, when I returned last night and found that my idiot brother had taken you out in a storm, that I'd probably lost you forever, I went completely mad. I told my parents how I felt about you. When Petra saw me carry you home in my arms, she finally agreed to go with Niko to Athens."

"Angela! Angela! Where are you?" Stephanie stood in front of the house, calling. "Mother has just told me everything! About you and Alex! Oh, Angela, I'm so happy! Oh, where are you?"

"Angela, Angela," came the shrill voices of the children, echoing their aunt.

"Come here, Angelika," said Alex, smiling wickedly as he concealed them both behind a tree.

"But Alex, they're calling—"

"Let them. I want another moment alone." He smiled. "Mother has known from the very beginning how it would be with us, although she said nothing. Mother has been content to use her very good mind and uncanny perceptions in the traditional female way."

"Oh, and am I expected to behave the same?" Angela asked him, smiling.

"Of course," he replied playfully. "You may have all

191

the independence you wish—as long as you always give in to me."

"Then I will have to travel everywhere with you, in order to do your bidding," she said, a tantalizing smile playing about the corners of her mouth. She finally understood that Alex was merely teasing her.

"Damn right you will travel with me. I'm not such a traditional Greek fool as to leave you at home. You know very well that I respect your independent spirit. No other kind of woman is worth having. As long as you do not make me jealous with another man. In that event I'm afraid I would be very Greek indeed."

Angela gazed lovingly at him, knowing he need have no fear on that score, ever.

Drawing closer to her, the dangerous look in his eyes once again, he grazed her bare arms with the tips of his fingers, sending a delicious tremor through her. "So, I remind you of Apollo?" His dazzling smile made her blush and lower her eyes.

"Don't be embarrassed, darling. I take it as a compliment. There are worse gods I could resemble. As for you, my wonderful Angelika, to me you have always been Aphrodite, the goddess of beauty and love."

"But—but Apollo had no connection with Aphrodite," Angelica objected in a shy whisper.

"Not until now," Alex murmured, taking her into his arms.